Estepona, 25th of
For Jean and all my love.

Flavia

KILLARI

By Flavia Z.B. Companys

This novel is dedicated to my husband, Louis Companys, who encouraged me to write the stories I had related to him regarding the culture of Peru, the country of my birth. His persistence over the past years finally convinced me, and I have now put this passionate story in print.

Special Thanks

A special thank you to Leo Ugarte, for creating the cover art for this book, and for advising me on various Quechua terms used throughout this book. Additionally, his attentive reading was a great help in providing the perspective I used in this work, that of the Andean people of the time.

Another thanks to Marilia Raez Villa Garcia and Katherine Chauvin, who read the novel with a great deal of enthusiasm and encouraged me to publish.

I would like to mention my former student Brooke Griffis who did the hard work to translate the novel from Spanish into English.

A special thanks for Carol Brooks who edited the English translation of this novel. She not only reflected the true spirit of this story but gave it a unified literary voice and feeling in her understanding and love of the culture.

A very special thanks goes to my son, Emmanuel, for supporting me to continue my adventure in literary creation.

Comments

<<In Flavia Companys' story she combines the mystery and magic surrounding the Andean culture with the patina of the legend, where the central figure, Killari emerges, who in my opinion represents the tenacity, intelligence and beautiful simplicity of the Peruvian woman, who can guide ventures without abandoning their essence, and be a genuine companion ready to sacrifice for the sake of loyalty >>.
Leo Ugarte — Historian and Painter. Arequipa.

<<Reading Killari made me recall our legends. It is a hymn to Peru with beautiful descriptions of Cusco and the triumph of love>>.
Marilia Ráez Villa García. Doctor of Language and Literature, Pontifical Catholic University of Peru.

<<Killari is a great story and a great read. I enjoyed it immensely>>.
Katharin Chauvin, Language Consultant for Rice University.

<<In the story of Killari, Flavia Companys made this period of her country's past come alive with this tale of the Inca people, told from their own perspective, while remaining true to the history of the period >>.
Carol Brooks. Entrepreneur - President, Moving Matters. LLC

Chapter 1

A beautiful girl was born on the day dedicated to the Moon Goddess (Mama Killa)[1]. She was the daughter of the *Coya*[2], Rahua Ocllo, wife of the Inca Emperor. The child was surrounded by the best caregivers, fed with quinoa water, bathed in corn water and dressed in the finest cotton from the Viru Valley. The Empire's High Priest interpreted the moon-shaped birthmark on the center of her chest as an indication that her name should be, Killari, which means «moonlight» in honor of the Moon Goddess.

Killari grew up in the city of Cusco, which Tahuantinsuyo Incas believed to be the birthplace of the world. She was taught by the best *amautas*[3], masters of the Inca Empire, who educated her on the traditions of her people. She had a natural aptitude for horticulture, with a special interest in flowers, especially the jungle orchids. Each day, she was accompanied by her soft, white pet alpaca whom she called Puquy, meaning «mature». The two loved to spend time both in the valleys and climbing the imposing heights of the Andes Mountains.

The young girl had two brothers. The elder, Unay was the first-born son of the Emperor and was heir to the throne. The other brother, whom she had never met, was Tinkupuma, the son of the Emperor's concubine, and was known for his military prowess. Unay on the contrary, detested war and anything related to the military. He had been educated in Cusco and trained to lead that part of the Empire. This brother really loved his sister, but was gone

---
[1] Mama Killa: Quechua for Mother Moon.
[2] Coya: Quechua for queen or principal wife of the Emperor.
[3] Amauta: Quechua for teacher.

for long periods, traveling to various villages of the Empire's four *suyos*[4]. Consequently, they seldom saw each other, but when he returned, he brought his sister pets from the regions of the Tahuantinsuyo, including a parrot from the East, and a little black puppy from the North, barely six months old, that Unay said was a VIringo (Northern dialect for <<dog>>). Killari named it Kusi[5], descriptive of it's joyful, and playful nature. This dog became Killari's protector and another dedicated companion.

Killari's greatest passion was climbing the mountains, especially the volcanoes, where she would encounter her friends, the condors. A small, select group would follow her closely to protect her from any danger. In this group was a young soldier, Anku, who was tall, thin, very strong, and was a specialist in mountain climbing. He could deal with the condors, and battle pumas. Under penalty of death, these companions were forbidden to speak with Killari.

---

[4] Suyos: Counties or regions of the Inca Empire.
[5] Kusi: Quechua for happy.

Chapter 2

On a June day, prior to Princess Killari's fifteenth birthday, she decided to journey from Cusco to Arequipa and climb the Misti and Chachani volcanoes with her group of companions. Both volcanoes had snow-capped peaks, but Misti especially, was covered with a white blanket that almost completely covered it, and its beauty was breathtaking. The valley of Arequipa was fertile and green; every variety of tuber, fruit, and vegetable was cultivated there. Houses were constructed of volcanic rock that was brought from the quarry near the city.

From Arequipa, the group journeyed on to the spectacular Colca Canyon, where, from the lookout point, they could enjoy the vista of Mismi's snowcapped ridge, with its incomparable white peaks. Inca lore indicated that this was the origin of the Great River.

Killari had been told that at Colca Canyon she might be able to see the largest condors in all the Empire. When they arrived at the summit, they saw two condors that closed in quickly on the princess. Everyone thought the worst—that one of the condors might attack Killari. She, however, advised her entourage not to intervene. One of the condors came very close to her, and without hesitation, she climbed on top of the bird. Anku was shocked to see that the condor unfolded its wings and carried the Princess through the air, crossing the great precipice of Colca. She smiled and shouted at the group assuring them that she would return. Many hours passed and Killari arrived back quite content. Her black hair was wet and glistening; her cheeks were rosy, and her face sported a lustrous appearance. She addressed the group with a firm voice:

- Do not tell anyone about any of this experience, under penalty of exile from the Empire.

When Killari reached the Royal Palace in the Valley of Arequipa, the women in attendance informed her that the Emperor had ordered her return to Cusco immediately. The trip lasted several days, with the companions transporting the princess on a royal palanquin.

During the trip to Cusco, Killari overheard a conversation that was of great interest to her. Anku was speaking to a young lady about the flight of the Princess on the condor.

- I would give my life to know from the Princess's own mouth what she saw, and above all, the experiences she had flying on the back of the condor.

- That's easy, Anku, said the young lady. Ask her yourself, and then afterwards, since they'll have to kill you for talking to her, you will have given your life for her. What we can't know is whether she will even answer your question or not.

Killari waited until nightfall after hearing this conversation, and then ordered Anku to visit her in her tent.

- Anku, I heard that you want to know details about my flight on the condor, she said.

Anku was kneeling with his head lowered in front of Killari.

- Lift your head and look at me, she declared authoritatively.

Anku obeyed, a little bewildered.

- I will tell you everything I remember. It was the first time I flew on the back of a condor. I have never felt surer of anything in my life. The condor flew toward the Misti volcano and from that height I saw the city of Arequipa. Since I was wrapped in my vicuña blanket, I wasn't cold. I felt as if I were welded to the condor's feathers. The clouds we went through were like cotton, and the most surprising of all was the conversation I had with the bird. It told me that the Moon Goddess had blessed me so that I will be happy, that I would help my family to stay united, and that the Empire of the Tahuantinsuyo would remain intact thanks to me. «Listen to your heart, always», was the last thing it told me.

Anku could not respond to the Princess, but a beautiful smile lit up his face out of gratitude for Killari's intimate confession.

- Thank you for listening to me, Anku. From now on you will be my friend and confidant. You must follow the rules when we are among the others, but when we are alone you may speak with me.

Anku left the tent feeling quite happy. He could not believe what was happening. For the first time, the Princess had spoken with him personally. Indeed, it was as if there were a special sweetness in the tone of her voice.

Chapter 3

When she arrived in Cusco, Killari's mother told her that a war had broken out between her brothers, initiated by Tinkupuma, with an army numbering in the thousands. They had traveled from Quito, in the north of the Empire, to confront Unay. In addition to this conflict, there was more bad news for Killari. Her father had returned to Cusco very ill, suffering from an unidentified new disease which had already become a plague in many parts of the Empire. Everyone was sure that it came from the north of the Tahuantinsuyo.

Unay decided to hide far from Cusco, intending to avoid a war for which he was not prepared; moreover, he understood it would be his war to lose. He skillfully left no trace of his whereabouts when he departed.

When he was twelve years old, Unay's father had taken him to a city that was still under construction. In fact, his grandfather had secretly begun its construction without disclosing its location. As the Emperor's elder son, Unay, of course, was the successor to the Empire. The Emperor had not considered dividing the Empire between his sons, Unay and Tinkupuma and he placed the responsibility on Unay to finish the construction of this city when he was old enough to do so. When Unay realized that Tinkupuma was an aggressive and ambitious rival, he decided to go first to the location where many of the secret city workers lived, called Patallaqta. From there he traveled to the hidden city.

This fortress of a city was finished quickly with the participation of a thousand bricklayers who were experts in carving granite and using age-old construction techniques of the Andes. The city had everything, especially a temple to worship the Sun God, Intihuatana at the highest point of the city, and a temple dedicated to the Moon Goddess. The priest named the city Machu Picchu, which means Old Mountain.

From then on, Unay planned the defense of the great Empire of Tahuantinsuyo, without getting involved in a bloody, senseless war. Since nobody was to reveal the location of the city, the bricklayers and other craftsmen had to swear an oath of confidentiality, not to divulge the site of its creation. Machu Picchu would be the heart of the four suyos: the Chinchasuyo, region of the northeast, also called the region of the puma; the Antisuyo in the eastern mountain ridges, or the region of the jaguar; the Continsuyo or the region of the condor, which extended from the western mountain ridge to the coast; and the last one, the Collasuyo, which comprised the south of the Empire and was also called the region of the llama.

Chapter 4

Three years passed, and Killari had become a beautiful young lady of marriageable age and the Emperor had a spousal candidate for his beloved daughter. He was Suri, a great sportsman and excellent runner, son of an ancient noble family of Cusco. The tradition of arranged marriages was a one that young people had always accepted, but Killari did not acknowledge this practice. She had set her sights on Anku, but nobody was aware of her feelings for the young soldier, including her mother, who had boasted that she knew all of her daughter's thoughts. Killari thought she might marry him one day, but she knew intuitively that she was going to have to confront some big issues. Although she was preparing herself physically and mentally to help maintain the Empire intact, she also understood that the animosity between her brothers would bring some serious problems.

Many groups that had only recently become part of the Inca Empire wanted to separate themselves from it, and they showed a willingness to fight like warriors in order to be free. Killari knew that in many places the *ayllus*[6] had managed to assimilate some groups into the Quechua culture, the culture of the Incas, but there were still many other groups that would not accept it. Killari constantly had these sorts of conversations with the *amautas*, her teachers, who helped keep her informed of the true situation of the Empire.

Unay's greatest dream was to bring his mother and sister to live with him in Machu Picchu. In order for that to happen, he had to

---

[6] Ayllus - Groups of families in the Inca Empire that worked the land together and shared their belongings, as in a commune. All people of the Empire belonged to an ayllu.

devise the perfect plan without his father, the Emperor, finding out. Unay knew that his half-brother Tinkupuma was traveling to Cusco to visit with their father to convince him to give him the right to the throne. Unay did not want to risk his mother and sister becoming prisoners of Tinkupuma and knew he had to bring them secretly to his new remote city. Unay discovered, through his messengers, that Killari was surrounded by a select group that accompanied her day and night. He also learned that Anku was responsible for them. Unay had to make contact with him and convince the soldier to obey his orders to execute the plan of moving his mother and Killari.

Unay's trusted man was undercover in Cusco. His name was Kallpa. It took no time, for him to contact Anku and arrange to meet with him on the outskirts of the city of Cusco, in the fortress of Sacsayhuaman.

- You don't know me, but I already know everything about you. I have come to propose something that you cannot refuse. Prince Unay has sent me. I cannot tell you where he is. You just have to follow my instructions. In exactly one week, you must bring Princess Killari and her mother here. In order to do that, you must sedate them with a special brew. For this I will supply you with the right herbs. One of the women who attends the royal family is in contact with us and she will prepare the concoction for the hour the Princess and her mother normally drink *maté* before going to bed. I will explain the rest in detail later.

- I do not know who you are. I have never met you before, but what you are asking me to do is prohibited, and if they discover me, they will kill me and my family.

- I understand that, Anku. Your family will have to leave immediately, to a secret hidden site. Prince Unay will not accept <<no>> for an answer. In fact, if you do not obey, you will be executed, and we will find another way to carry out our plan.

- Then, I suppose there is nothing left but to accept. I must say, that I am honored that Prince Unay has chosen me for this mission.

- You will be very well received where we are going, and you will be reunited with your family there. You cannot let anyone know about our plan. We will contact you soon to give you further instructions.

Anku returned immediately to the royal palace where Killari was living, without raising any alarms. He later received his instructions by way of a messenger who explained the escape plan to the Hidden City in great detail.

In Machu Picchu, the entire city was preparing to receive Prince Unay's mother and his sister Killari. The Temple of the Sun had been finished. The grand inauguration ceremony for the city was to be celebrated there, including worship of the Sun God Inti, the all-powerful, whom everyone was required to worship, to revere, and to show obedience as well. The priest, and maidens who were dedicated solely to the religious rites, were trained in the *Acllahuasi*[7] to help the priest step by step. These maidens were never to marry, and their position in society was considered a great honor for their families.

---

[7] Acllahuasi - Quechua for centers of cloistered, educated, chosen women, devoted to the religion.

Chapter 5

Prince Tinkupuma was born in Quito to the Emperor's favorite concubine, Tamaya, a gorgeous woman who had completely subjugated the Emperor. Tinkupuma adored his mother and always followed her advice willingly. She was an ambitious woman and strived for her only son to inherit the throne. Tinkupuma, in total accord, hoped that his father would support his plans of war against his brother Unay. Instead, the Emperor disagreed, and preferred peace between the two brothers. To this end, the Emperor traveled from Quito to Cusco in an effort to convince Unay to meet with his brother, as he was considering dividing the Empire in two: Tinkupuma would rule Quito and Cusco would go to Unay.

During this trip, the Emperor fell ill with a sickness never before seen in the Empire. One of his sons who was accompanying him on the journey, also became sick. They arrived in Cusco and received the best care that could be accorded royalty.

The preparations for Tinkupuma's arrival in Cusco had all the residents of the Imperial City very busy. As a matter of fact, this distraction would help Unay's plan to move his mother and sister. Unay had the plan well-organized and nothing could go wrong. That very night, the plan would be put into action.

The night was quite dark, since there was no radiant moon to light the way, which might have interfered. Killari's mother drank her prepared *maté*, and Killari drank hers a few moments later. They both fell deeply asleep. Killari dreamed of an endless journey through the night, passing through Urubamba and arriving at a mountain she had never seen before. The city was impressive, with an endless number of stairways and corridors, and ample vegetation. She saw her dog Kusi running joyfully throughout the city. She followed him restlessly, exploring this precious city suspended in the air, surrounded by clouds…

Anku placed Killari and her mother in two giant baskets, normally used to transport the palace bedclothes. They were deeply asleep and were unaware of these events. The narcotic brew was strong enough to last the whole trip. The baskets left the palace without any problem. Anku and his group mounted the baskets on top of two llamas, and they started the journey to Machu Picchu with the help of General Kallpa.

To get to the hidden city, they had to traverse approximately 75 kilometers on foot. They would pass through several cities such as Chinchero, Maras, and Ollantaytambo, until they arrived at the thermal pools.

Then they reached the village of Qorihuayrachina and from that point on they found themselves experiencing varying elevations and climates, from the Andean plains to the cloud forests. One area of exceptional height was Warmiwañusca, at 4,200 meters. It was difficult to climb the steep path as quickly as they had anticipated, but somehow, they managed.

The trip was not at all as easy as they had hoped. The rain fell heavily, and they had to find shelter in different <<*tambos*>> along the way. (A tambo was a structure that was meant primarily for storing food.) The journey took place during the middle of November, and rain was beginning to fall almost daily.

They spent the first night in Llullucha. On the second day they climbed up to 4,200 meters, and then dropped down to the valley where the Pakaymayu River flowed.

The third day found them climbing again up the path toward Runkurakay until they reached a height of 3,800 meters and they subsequently arrived at the magnificent lake of Yanacocha, the Black Lake. They could finally rest and have a meal in Sayaqmarca, a village with narrow streets, many buildings such as sanctuaries, patios, and canals, on various levels, as well as a great exterior wall. Anku took the opportunity to visit the temple and the city's astronomical observatory. They were able to stock up on water and food that they found in a great *tambo*, exclusively used for food storage. At that point, Killari and her mother were still asleep, unaware of the long journey toward the Hidden City.

When they arrived at Wiñay Wayna, the Princess was the first to awaken. As she opened her eyes, she noticed that everything was dark, and she did not recognize her surroundings. Killari realized that she was wrapped in a vicuña blanket and could barely move; she did not understand what was happening. Her first reaction was to call out so someone could come to help her,

- Get me out of here! Help! Please, come! Killari yelled.

They removed her from the basket but the only one she recognized was Anku. Who were these other people?

- Princess Killari, we are on a journey ordered by your brother Unay and we cannot delay any longer. We have promised him that we will be there in two more days. Let me introduce you to your brother's messenger, the general Kallpa, said Anku hastily.

- Am I traveling without my family? the princess asked.

- No. Your mother has not yet awakened. This would be a good time to open the basket and see how she is, said the general.

- My mother? I do not believe it. She would never abandon the palace.

- She does not know about this journey. We had to rescue you both while you were asleep, under orders from your brother. He wants to protect you from your other brother, Tinkupuma, who is on his way to Cusco. Unay is convinced that Tinkupuma would have made you prisoners in the Royal Palace of Cusco.

- It seems strange to me that my brother would not speak to me directly before planning the trip. My father will be very worried about us if he does not hear from us, Killari said. Then she asked the general, Where are we?

- In Wiñay Wayna, Princess, responded Kallpa.

- I want to stretch my legs. They feel stiff, complained Killari.

- Go with the Princess, said Kallpa, directing his command to Anku.

- Yes sir, General, Anku obeyed.

They distanced themselves a bit from the group of travelers, and Killari became aware of the change in vegetation. They climbed up as high as they could, and from there they could view the city constructed out of stone and further down, the Urubamba River. Suddenly Killari spied a beautiful carmine-red orchid.

- Look at how beautiful that is! Killari exclaimed.

- Yes, it is called the <<Wiñay Wayna>>. It means, <<forever young>>, and it gives the name to this city.

- The paths are beautiful in this part of our land. It is clear that the farmers love this *Pachamama*, our mother earth, and she responds to their love with abundant harvests.

- That is right. We have gathered enough food here for the days left in our journey before we arrive at the city where we will join your brother.

- Let's walk a little more to see what else we can find.

They came to a place filled with flora, and there were numerous other different, and colorful orchids. Killari counted them and there were approximately three hundred varieties of orchids. The birds were innumerable too, including precious hummingbirds and <<painted>> butterflies.

- I have never seen a place like this. It is like a heavenly paradise.

Suddenly they heard the roar of an animal. Anku prepared himself to spring into action to defend the princess. It was a bear on its hind legs appearing to be at least six feet tall. It was the Andean bear, sometimes known as the spectacled bear because of the big black markings around its eyes. Anku preferred not to kill it and decided the best thing to do would be to leave very slowly, without provoking the animal. It climbed a nearby tree in search of food. Then Killari and Anku quickly returned to the group.

All at once they heard shouting from the other basket. They opened it and extricated Killari's mother. When they got her to her feet on the saturated ground, all the companions bowed down in a gesture of respect for the Emperor's wife.

Mother and daughter embraced. There was no need to explain anything.

- I have already heard the conversation among the people who are accompanying us. My daughter and I will cooperate completely in order to reunite with Unay as soon as possible.

Killari heard the barking of her dog, Kusi, and saw her adored alpaca, Puquy, not far away. She was comforted knowing her dear friends were still with her on this journey.

The caravan started out once more after having fed both Killari and her mother. The scenery began to change. There was an ever-increasing amount of vegetation. The climate was humid and very sunny producing extreme heat during the day. The men who led the way cleared the path with long machetes, cutting their way through the thick undergrowth. The three days of intense walking were accompanied by abundant rain, which made the trek even more difficult.

They saw many indigenous animals in that area. They saw <<*tunki*>>, the cock-of-the-rock, a precious bird with intense red plumes on its head, neck, and back, an extensive cape of gray, and an underlying layer of black feathers. They also saw the Andean fox prowling around nearby. They spied a puma not far from the path, and they had to prepare themselves to fight it, but then fortunately, were able to kill a deer to feed and distract the puma, allowing them to pass. The group came across many other mountain animals, like caracaras, parrots, wild ducks, reptiles, and serpents. Killari frequently asked the names of the new animals and repeated them all to herself so that she would not forget them.

Chapter 6

The journey to Machu Picchu was a very comfortable one for Killari and her mother. They had traveled eight kilometers through the jungle and were welcomed miles before the entrance to the citadel. They arrived at an area of hot springs where some women took charge of bathing them, using earthenware jars filled with hot water, and then dressing them. Killari and her mother were settled into a special palanquin called a *hantu* to carry them up the mountain. Teams of men took turns carrying them, allowing the ascent to be completed with ease. When they arrived at the mountaintop, Killari was able to survey the precious city. They were at the magical entrance of the *Inti Punku*, or Sun Gate. Killari was ecstatic, beholding this marvelous city hung in the heavens and surrounded by clouds. The great mountain of Huayna Picchu was in front of them, as if it were greeting the new arrivals to this enchanted place. The city seemed like it was drawn into the mountain, covering every usable space. The stone buildings were well-built with the pulchritude and precision of the Andean bricklayers. Killari intoned:

- Great Gods, I do not know whether this is a piece of heaven on earth, or a piece of earth in the heavens.

She recognized the city she had seen in her dreams and thought: <<When dreams become reality, I think that I am sleeping, and I am afraid to wake up>>.

The handmaidens had readied the royal bedchamber for the Princess and her mother, for they needed to be properly prepared before they could present themselves in front of Unay. Their bathing ceremony included massage with essential oils, elaborate hairstyling, dresses made of fine, colorful cotton, and above all gold and silver jewelry created by gifted jewelry craftsmen.

At the conclusion of these rituals, two maidens announced that Prince Unay was waiting for them in the royal sitting room.

Upon entering the room, Killari saw her brother Unay seated on a great throne, accompanied by General Kallpa and several men she did not know. Unay approached his mother, who received him with a great blessing. She looked at him tenderly and said,

- I understand that you have had to make this decision to be close to your people. Right now, we would be in the hands of Tinkupuma, separated from you forever, under the control of his mother, the concubine Tamaya. She cares only about her son and power for herself and her family. Your father only listens to what she desires; she has had him bewitched for a long time, and besides that, he is ill.

- Yes, mother, I know. And you, dear sister? You have become a splendid orchid, like one of those in your collection.

- Do not judge me by my appearance, Unay. I want you to know me just as I am. I want to collaborate in your government to strengthen the Tahuantinsuyo. Let me explore this place to understand its possibilities and limitations. I want to meet all the women here, learn the regional plants, know what they cook, and meet the *amautas* and their schools.

- My goodness, Killari. You talk like a leader. I was not aware of your great curiosity about our people's government. I accept your help, Unay responded.

- Your sister has received the best education from our *amautas*. She has traveled a lot, though not as much as you. Nevertheless, she knows many plants and animals, and she adores children, said their mother.

- I hope I can help you, Unay. We have to be united now that Tinkupuma is going to arrive in Cusco ready to crown himself with his own hands, leaving our father in a humiliating situation, said Killari, worried.

- That is right. And he will arrive, accompanied by his mother, who thirsts for riches and power, added the Empress.

- We have to pray to the God Inti and to the Moon Goddess so that they will protect us, declared Killari.

- Tomorrow there will be a major ceremony in the Sanctuary of the Sun. Our High Priest has everything prepared, said Unay.

- Killari and I will be ready to pray for the health of the Tahuantinsuyo, declared their mother with conviction.

General Kallpa was also a skilled engineer and had participated in the construction of the City of Machu Picchu. He offered to personally guide Killari and her mother, the *Coya* Rahua Ocllo, around the city.

- This city has been designed to worship our gods. The Royal Palace is in the center and is very spacious and comfortable, and its ceilings are a bit higher. There are three temples and a place to worship the Sun God, our eternal Intihuana the holy one, who shows us the exact position of the sun during the Solstice.

- What are the names of the temples? Killari asked.

- The Temple of Three Windows, the Temple of the Condor, and the Sacred Rock, where we honor our devotion to the mountains, the general explained.

- Do the children attend school?

- Yes, they go to where the *amautas* of this city live. There is also another location where the stones are still being worked.

- How have you managed to get water?

- Not too far from here, to the north of the city, there are some natural waterfalls that have been rerouted with canals directing water toward the city. Water is also one of our main deities. The city has a total of sixteen liturgical fountains, or *packchas*, which form a path between the Temple of the Sun and the Royal Palace.

- Thank you, General Kallpa, for sharing your knowledge, but soon we will need to be ready for the religious ceremony, Killari interrupted.

The ceremony in honor of the god Inti was impressive. The great priest Willac Umu led the ceremony, dressed in red and adorned with various feathers. Unay was seated on the royal throne facing the stone of the Intihuatana. He was draped with a vicuña fleece which covered his whole body and his head was adorned with a royal headdress.

Everyone in Machu Picchu wanted Unay to succeed his father as the Emperor of the Tahuantinsuyo and to see him adorned in all the regalia of the Incas.

Chapter 7

The palace in Cusco was on high alert. The disappearance of the Emperor's wife and Killari had provoked a situation of confusion. Nobody knew any details about how it had happened, however they knew that Anku had participated because he was nowhere to be found, and neither was the little group that operated under his command. They went looking for his family, who lived in the Urubamba Valley, but they could not find anyone.

The news reached Machu Picchu a few weeks later. The Emperor, as well as his son who had accompanied him continued to be gravely ill in Cusco and nobody knew anything about this illness that produced high fevers and pustules all over the body. The Emperor found it hard to accept the disappearance of his wife and his beloved daughter. Meanwhile, Tinkupuma had arrived in Cusco accompanied by his mother. Everyone was prepared to learn the worst news, the Emperor's death.

Tinkupuma's mother tended to the Emperor and called the High Priest so that the Emperor could designate his successor. The Emperor said:

- We must contact Unay as soon as possible so that he will know that he will be declared Emperor here in Cusco before I die. Tinkupuma will be Emperor in Quito, where he will reign for the protection of the Empire, with his army of more than 50,000 soldiers.

- There is no way of speaking with him. He has disappeared completely. He does not want to confront his brother. He prefers to avoid this brotherly war that he would lose, since war is not to his liking, responded the priest.

- Then we have no option but to crown Tinkupuma as Emperor of the Tahuantinsuyo. Prepare the ceremony. It will take place before my death. That is my last wish.

- So, it will be, My Lord, said the priest. Call Tinkupuma's mother.

Tamaya presented herself to the Emperor. Her beauty was overwhelming—her ambition even more so. The Emperor told her to come close.

- Our son's coronation will take place tomorrow. The *Maskaypacha* is ready for the High Priest to crown him. He must be prepared tonight for tomorrow's big ceremony.

- *Viracocha*[8] has heard my prayers. Tomorrow my deepest wish will be fulfilled. I hope our ancestors will bless you for your just decision. You will be proud of your son.

- The Tahuantinsuyo created by my father in such a short time cannot lose with this little conflict. We must fight against time. I will ask *Viracocha* to receive me in the Sun. I leave your son to you so you can guide him. Try to convince him to find peace with his brother Unay. Take care of him.

The Emperor died that same night. He could not be present at the ceremony to see the high priest give the *Maskaypacha* to his favorite son.

The body of the Emperor was embalmed using the accepted Inca science and according to the funeral traditions of the Empire's leader. The Emperor had asked that his heart be sent to Quito where it would be close to his family who had lived there. He also

---

[8] Viracocha - Supreme god of the Incas and considered the creator god, the father of all other Inca gods who formed the earth, heavens, sun, moon and all living beings.

asked that his mummified body remain in the Temple of the Sun in the city of Cusco. His body would be looked after, so that it might be transported in front of the people on the day of Inti Raymi, the 24th of June. The new Emperor would also attend the rites that day, which were of great importance to his people. The Emperor's youngest son died two days later.

The noble families of Cusco attended the ceremony, afraid of the possible retaliations on the part of the new Emperor Tinkupuma if they were not present. They would have preferred Unay, who belonged to a royal family of Cusco and had already reigned with maximum authority there, while the now deceased Emperor spent long periods in Quito. The funeral ceremony took place in the Temple of Coricancha. Tamaya was dressed in a white suit and wore a large red cape. A lock of her hair had been cut from her head as a sign of grief for her husband. A solid gold necklace adorned her neck and her hair had been braided with golden threads. Everyone in the temple watched her with admiration and fear. Tinkupuma received the *Maskaypacha*, a crown with a fine red tassel, encrusted with golden thread and feathers of the mountain caracara. He had become the Intiq Churin, the reigning Emperor.

Chapter 8

After a while informant took the news to Unay, the *Auqui*, rightful heir apparent to the throne. Unay was in conversation with his sister when the *chasqui*[9], who was coming from Cusco, entered with the news.

- The Emperor died the night before last. Yesterday Tinkupuma was crowned *Intiq Churin* in the Temple of Coricancha. The entire royal family attended the coronation and now Tinkupuma's mother is the *Coya* of the Empire.

- You should have something to eat and stay the night here. You will take a return message to my family tomorrow.

- Killari embraced Unay, crying. Our father has died, and he was replaced immediately! Tamaya's deepest desire has finally come true. Tinkupuma will not stop until he finds our hiding place, Killari exclaimed between tears.

- Our father's death upsets me tremendously, said Unay in a quivering voice. We will have to strengthen our city and keep it isolated from any other paths of the Tahuantinsuyo.

Just then the mother of Unay and Killari entered. She was calm, but her sadness was visible on her face, and her children knew that she had already heard the news of her husband's tragic death.

---

[9] Chasqui - An official runner who was agile, highly trained and physically fit, and who carried messages and gifts using a relay system.

- Thank you, Unay, for protecting us. Killari and I would be prisoners in Cusco right now if it were not for you.

- Mother, you have no need to thank me. I am happy to have you both at my side. Now we must protect ourselves from Tinkupuma's claws.

- May our gods protect us, said the *Coya* Rahua Ocllo with a trembling voice. Killari hugged her mother and they cried together, mourning the Emperors's death.

Several months passed, and the news from Cusco was alarming. Many noble families of Cusco had abandoned the city on Tinkupuma's orders, and in their place were the *ayllus* from Quito, who arrived to occupy the noble residences. Some families had been declared traitors and killed along with all their servants. Tamaya, the new *Coya* of the Empire, was surrounded by a group of maidens who were entirely at her service.

Chapter 9

Anku was still Killari's protector and companion. Killari wanted to travel to the East of the Tahuantinsuyo because its jungle, although known to the Incas, was still pristine, but also to construct a shelter in the event Tinkupuma discovered the new city of Machu Picchu. She knew he would be unforgiving of Unay and probably with herself, as well.

She asked Unay's permission to go on this exploration trip, accompanied by Anku and a small group of companions who had come from Cusco with them. The group was comprised of eight men who knew the secrets of the jungle, and five women solely to attend Killari. Anku would be the leader of the expedition, and Killari would have the ultimate authority. They left Cusco Province heading north, looking for significant rivers leading to the Great River that resembled a sea. Anku and Killari knew that this trip would last for months. To this end, they had constructed suitable light rafts for navigating the mighty river. Kusi, the dog, went along with them. The most difficult aspect of the journey was negotiating the large rivers that led down to the jungle. They had to travel during the months historically known to have no rain so they could traverse the rivers more easily, as the currents were less strong during dry seasons. They spent the nights under a royal camping tent shielding them from the animals and insects. They had been warned of a deadly mosquito-borne disease, so they drank a <<quinine>> based beverage made from the bark of the <<chinchona tree>> to protect themselves. When they arrived at an island of considerable size located on the Great River, they realized that it was inhabited by a small tribe. Its chief introduced them to a shaman, who invited them to stay as long as they cared to.

Killari was surprised to see the number of unique birds of every imaginable color and size. The shaman asked them in perfect Quechua who they were and what they were doing in the jungle. Killari simply mentioned that they were escaping from the war that was about to start and that they were seeking a peaceful place to situate themselves. The island chief did not speak Quechua, so they were only able to communicate through the shaman. The Chief also invited them to stay as long as they desired.

From that island, Killari and Anku explored the area to familiarize themselves with the nearby sites, in an attempt to find an appropriate place where they might settle down. The shaman offered to accompany them to keep them from getting lost in the maze of the Great River's tributaries. One day, they found themselves at a site that had thick mats of vegetation and decided this would be a perfect place. There were some waterfalls that brought an energy to the area, and not too far away they found a plethora of orchids of every color. Killari had indeed found a place in which she wanted to settle. They named that place <<Suyakuy>>, which means Hope.

The shaman asked them if they cared to explore the place where the pink dolphins lived. Killari accepted the offer enthusiastically. They set out early in a canoe, and when they arrived, they saw unusual pink dolphins leaping from the water in an apparent ballet. Anku asked if he could touch the dolphins, and the shaman informed him that they were not domesticated, however the dolphins sometimes communed with humans, so they could try. Killari asked Anku if he could teach her to swim. Anku was a great swimmer and in just a few days Killari was also able to swim and enjoy the water. From that day forward, Killari communed and swam with the pink dolphins, who would nudge her feet, propelling her to travel short distances quickly. Anku and Killari enjoyed this activity together, and each day they grew closer.

The jungle was a real box of surprises. There was not a day that Killari did not find something new. One afternoon, on one of their walks, they found a small cave with a jaguar cub. Killari had never seen an animal that beautiful. She was told that she would not be able to keep it, because these animals could not be trained.

- I will domesticate him, and nobody can take him away from me. He will be my companion and protector.

- I will help you, Princess, said Anku affectionately.

A few months passed, and the jaguar cub grew into a magnificent beast. Killari called him *Rumi*, meaning <<rock>>. At first Kusi, her dog, was quite jealous of Killari's new companion, but soon the two became inseparable.

The time came when the shaman asked Killari if she was interested in foreseeing the future. She responded that she was.

- We shall perform the Rite of Knowledge to prepare you. I will need to educate you in the arts of the Spirit. Are you ready to start this journey of spiritual adventure?

- What must I do?

- You will drink a tea made of the <<plant of knowledge>>. Afterward, your visions will portray the future and you must not be afraid. You will have to be strong, because some of the predictions will be very disturbing for your pure and tender soul.

- I am strong, and I can manage it. I also want Anku to be there.

- As you wish.

The ceremony started in the afternoon with a total cleansing of her body. Killari drank the brew and laid down on a bed that was prepared for the spiritual journey. Within a few hours, Killari sat up and began talking. She had a glazed look, but her words were perfectly coherent.

- What do you see? Where are you? the shaman asked her.

- I am on Lake Titicaca in a boat made of reeds. It is very cold. I can feel the cold air on my face. The lake's waters are blue, and the moonlight is reflected on the vast surface of the waters. I see a condor soaring alone over the lake. The condor picks me up and begins its flight so that I can view the enormous size of the lake. It talks to me in a calm voice:

- Here is where the Inca Empire was born, under the orders of Viracocha, our god, creator of everything that exists. In days gone by, there was a great valley full of vegetation and huge trees. The pumas lived there, sacred animals that protected this place against strangers. Then men came to the valley and had brother-killing wars to decide who would get to rule it. The god Viracocha, seeing all that death and destruction, cried so much that the valley filled with water and the pumas were turned into stone for all eternity. They are still there at the bottom of the lake. You must speak with Unay so that the same fate does not happen to the Inca Empire. You must convince him to never confront his brother Tinkupuma because he will kill him and destroy the Inca civilization. Then he, Tinkupuma, will turn into a puma of stone, and the condors will fling him to the bottom of Titicaca. Now I will take you to Cusco so that you can see everything that has happened.

- The condor is continuing its flight until he comes close to Cusco. Seeing it from a distance, and at a great height, I realize that the city has the perfect shape of a puma. It is nighttime and nobody can see us. The moon totally illuminates the city and I can see the Temple of Coricancha and the Temple of the Moon. I recognize the streets and buildings made of stone. Somehow, I can see through the walls to the people living there, and I can identify the Imperial Palace. I see Tinkupuma, too - the brother I never met. He seems very young, strong, and beautiful, but he does not have any light in his eyes; it is as if he were blind. He is lean and muscular. His hair is very full and long, very black, with a bluish luster. His mother is next to him, talking to him about a wedding. I have never seen a more beautiful woman in my life. Her body is perfectly proportioned, and her face is of Inca-beauty perfection. Still, there is something bothering me that, when I look at her, I cannot exactly describe, <<Yes, shaman, I am listening, and I am concentrating, but I still cannot see it very clearly>>. Oh, now, I see! There is a light behind her, and I can see a shadow, the profile of something monstrous, that watches over her and directs her. It is black and it has gray wings. Now I am inside the Temple of Coricancha where my father's body rests. He looks almost as if he were asleep, accompanied by his most loyal servants who wished to go with him to the great beyond. I feel very sad because I would have wanted to hug him and care for him until his death. I do not see anything now. I am tired and want to return. I am going to get ready to return to the jungle with you all.

Chapter 10

In Cusco, everything had changed. There were hardly any royal families of Cusco left. Many had been killed for disobeying the royal order to leave everything behind and exit the city. New families who came from Quito occupied the abandoned residences with their families. The flow of new people was constant.

In the Royal Palace, Tinkupuma repeatedly asked what had happened to his sister Killari and her mother, the *Coya*. All the servants had been interrogated, and many of them had been tortured, but no one had any answers.

Knowing that Unay had gone into hiding upset Tinkupuma, because he could not understand why he had allowed him to walk free in the first place. He knew that Unay hated war but had warriors who would defend him until the death. The newly crowned Emperor would have liked to have met his sister Killari, who, he understood, was just as pretty as she was intelligent.

Tinkupuma was supremely bored in the royal palace of Cusco. He decided to travel around the Sacred Valley and all the regions near the capital of the Empire. He enjoyed hunting and returning with all kinds of trophies. He had not chosen a wife, but his mother was taking care of that. Tinkupuma was very young, but his mother wanted to establish a line of descendants for him as quickly as possible. In this way, she could consolidate the factions and ensure her son's political power. Tamaya asked the advice of the High Priest, who counseled her to have her son marry a daughter of a noble family from Cusco. There were not many royal families left in in the city, but the deceased Emperor's' cousin was still living there, and he was very respected. His name was Pushaq, and he had a lovely daughter of marriageable age. An invitation was sent to Pushaq from the Palace, and he presented himself immediately. Tamaya received him, respecting all the protocol necessary for a person of his rank member of the royal family.

- Welcome, Tamaya said to him.

- Thank you for inviting me, said Pushaq.

- I want to be very direct in this meeting, my dear cousin. I have called you here to ask for your daughter's hand in marriage to my son, the Emperor.

- I am surprised... I thought he wanted to establish a new line of descendants with people from Quito.

- You thought wrong. I want to unite our different bloods to strengthen the empire. That was my deceased husband's dream, may he rest in peace.

- I feel honored. I am sure my family would, too. When do you desire this wedding to take place?

- As soon as possible. The union of the bride and groom must happen next week, when my son returns from his trip.

- We will do everything we can to welcome you into our home in the manner you deserve. Your presence honors us, *Coya*.

- Before you go, I would like to meet your daughter.

- Of course. I will summon her.

Some twenty minutes passed before they saw Pushaq's daughter. Her name was Kori. She appeared in a flattering white dress which made her look attractive and slim, with a well-proportioned face. Tamaya asked her to introduce herself. She was anxious to hear the girl's voice and study her personality. Kori said as little as possible and avoided Tamaya's gaze.

- What do you like to do? Tamaya asked.

- Weaving is the activity I do the most, and I enjoy it very much.

- Do you know how to play an instrument?

- I have played the *quena*[10] since I was a little girl.

- My son likes music, especially before he goes to sleep. Prepare something to play for him when he comes next week.

- I will do that, said Kori.

Tamaya was very impressed by Pushaq's family, particularly his daughter Kori, who would soon be her son's wife, and the most important woman in the Empire apart from herself. She preferred a younger woman for her son so that she could exercise control over her and this one seemed very docile. Besides, Kori was good-looking, so this girl also might be appealing to her son.

---

[10] Quena - The flute of the Andes.

Chapter 11

The day came for the future husband and wife to meet. Tinkupuma agreed to the appointment to meet his future wife because he blindly trusted his mother's judgement. The meeting was to take place in the Royal Palace of Cusco, since the Emperor preferred to remain within the palace for safety reasons. The Royal Palace was adorned with flowers and perfumes of essential oils thought to bring good luck to the couple. The first to arrive was the bride-to-be with her family. They waited a while for the arrival of the royal family but became anxious because they did not understand the delayed appearance of the Emperor and his mother. Finally, both sovereigns arrived along with a musical band. Kori was very nervous, but she presented a calm demeanor. Tinkupuma's face was expressionless when he saw the beautiful girl. He sat on his throne and invited the guests to sit around the table of honor. Tamaya began the conversation:

- Welcome to the Palace. My son the Emperor is very happy to meet you. Let us begin the festivities.

The music began, with *quenas*, shepherd's pipes, and several percussion instruments. Dancing maidens also performed, turning and twisting to the rhythms of the music. The walls were lined with gold-leaf, and priceless rugs covered the floor to impress the guests. Then came the trays of traditional Andean food: the best corn, potatoes of every size and color, *chicha*-based drinks which were brewed from fermented corn, fruits of every kind, especially eggfruit and custard apples, and plates full of fresh fish, which had just been brought from the coast at full speed by the *chasquis*, the fastest men in the empire.

Kori ate very little. She had no appetite, and she was distracted by the inquisitive gaze of the young Emperor. Her mother took notice of this and tried to cheer her up, taking her hand. The mother quietly complimented Kori, telling her how lovely she looked in her white dress, and that the jewels that accessorized it were just perfect for the outfit. Kori smiled a little to placate her mother. Still, it seemed unreal to her that she was actually sitting in the Emperor's Palace, about to become his wife in just a few days. Her life was about to change entirely, and of course nobody had asked her opinion about any of this. She was just sixteen years old and she was not yet considered an adult woman. She would have to leave her family's house and somehow become accustomed to being the wife of the most powerful man in the Empire. Kori's thoughts were filled with questions about her future: What would happen with her life? Her family? Her friendships? Her customs? Her feelings?

The party ended very late, and the Emperor asked to see Kori alone. They met one another in Tinkupuma's private quarters. Kori felt as if her heart would leap out of her throat. She tried to pretend to keep her composure, as he got closer to her.

- You do not have to fear of me. You are a gorgeous girl, Kori. In a few days you will be my wife and you will live with us in this Palace. You will be required to please me, no matter what I ask of you; that is the role of the Emperor's wife. You will have to give me descendants very soon, and I hope that all my plans will come about without any problems. I have been told that you play the *quena* very well. The day I ask you to play it, you should be prepared to perform for me.

Tinkupuma turned and left Kori alone, trembling in the middle of this great room. She could not imagine herself in an intimate situation with this man she had just met. He was a beautiful man, and very intelligent, but she did not have any romantic feelings for him, and she never would.

Chapter 12

Killari woke up very cold and tired. The shaman gave her another brew so she could sleep peacefully.

The next day, Killari called Anku,

- Get everything ready. Soon we will reunite with my brother and my mother. I want to take my jaguar with me, and all of my animals that will be able to survive in the altitude of Machu Picchu. Ask permission from the chief of the tribe to see if we might take those two children who are always following me around. They have learned so much Quechua already, and they will be happy on that old mountain.

The children received the news with surprise. Killari gave them new Quechua names that they truly liked. The boy was seven years old and he was called Pikichaqui, which means <<light-footed,>> and the girl was five years old and she was called Kukuri, which means <<dove.>> They were brother and sister, and they liked the idea of getting to know new places with Killari. Anku was very happy when he discovered the news. He enjoyed playing with the children and he taught them Quechua songs, which they sang as he played the *quena*. Anku was a great musician and he composed a beautiful song:

<<That voice emerging from within you,
That voice quivering inside of you...

Smooth and deep, it rings out.
Grave-robber memories
Of Andean clay
Latch onto it.

That voice emerging from within you
Is your voice quivering inside of you.

Sound of cotton
Texture of starch
Chords of harmony
Notes, notes of melancholy.

That voice emerging from within you
That voice quivering inside of you
It is your voice that invades my soul,
Your voice that makes me tremble.

Sacred coca leaf,
Seed of the Quechua people,
Incense of a found soul
I sing of your enchanted innocence.

That voice emerging from within you,
That voice quivering inside of you.

Velvet caresses,
Gazes of restless desire,
Memories of fiery skin
Your soul will always yearn for.

Stones of Machu Picchu
Heights of pure quartz
Strong-bodied Andeans
Eternal granite, in you I live on.

Sound of cotton,
Texture of starch,
Chords of harmony,
Notes, notes of melancholy

That voice emerging from within you... >>

Anku did not know that Killari was listening to his song. Therefore, he was able to sing the song from his heart, without any external interruption. Killari asked him:

- That song - who taught it to you?

- No one, Princess. I made it along with the help of my *quena*.

- And what is the title?

- Voices of Your Voice.

- And who were you thinking about when you wrote it?

- A-a-about my *quena*, Princess, Anku stuttered.

- Well, I can see you care about it quite a lot. Your *quena* is very lucky.

- Yes, it is true. I love it more than myself, said Anku very assuredly.

Pikichaqui and Kukuri listened to the song and started to sing it softly. Anku played his *quena* to help them with the melody. The children were very happy and Killari so enjoyed seeing them like that.

Killari had a very clear idea of Anku's feelings for her, and so did he about hers, but they never broached the topic. It was taboo. Killari felt she just had to do something about it, so she decided to tell her close friend and confidant about it.

- I want to ask you something, Amankay.

- Tell me, Princess.

- What do you think of Anku?

- Well, he is a nice young man. Why do you ask?

- You have known him for a few years. I want you to give me a more detailed opinion of him.

- He is brave, hardworking, he honors his name, and he is strong. He is very reserved, but he is also an artist. He composes beautiful songs and he knows how to play them. He is sincere and honest. He respects and admires you a lot.

- Admires? What do you mean by that?

- He always mentions how smart you are, and he says you are very decisive.

- Very well. Do you know if he is in love?

- He is very private. He has never told me anything so intimate.

- Do you think he likes me, as a woman?

- Princess, I wouldn't know something like that. You would have to ask him. And it seems to me that he would never dare to admit something like that to anyone. The only thing I can tell you is that he would give his life for you.

- Your opinion is very valuable to me, Amankay. Keep watching him and let me know what you notice.

- As you wish, Princess, Amankay replied, with an impish smile.

Chapter 13

Killari decided to return to Machu Picchu that very day. She took her jaguar and all the little animals she had found in the jungle: birds, monkeys, even some rodents. There were innumerable plants; she had learned the curative properties of the majority of them.

It took them two months to return to the Sacred Valley since they had to avoid being seen. Killari searched for condor nests to help guide her back to Machu Picchu. When she encountered a condor, she climbed onto its back. She was able to communicate with the condors through eye contact alone. Killari guided the bird to the Sacred City. Upon arrival, she felt a great joy because soon she would be reunited with her brother and her mother. She would get back to her old lifestyle and be able to dedicate herself to the cultivation of the plants that Anku and her group of companions were bringing from the journey. First, she met up with Unay:

- Dear sister, you've come home! I've missed you so much!

- I've found some new specimens in the jungle, and also I've found a place where we can settle down if Tinkupuma threatens to make us prisoners. And our mother? How is she?

- Unfortunately, her health has declined since you left.

- Where is she? I want to see her right now.

- I'll take you to her.

Killari's mother had aged a great deal in just a few months. She was sitting in front of one of the windows looking out at the morning sunlight. The doctors could not find any specific illness, but each day she was weaker.

Killari hugged her mother.

- I'm back, mother. I'll take care of you.

- I've missed you so much, Killari. These months have felt like years. How long ago did you return, and with whom?

- I've just come back. Anku and my group of companions will get back in a few days. We experienced some dangers but were very lucky.

- Viracocha, our god the Creator, has accompanied and protected you!

- I think you're right, mother.

When she left her mother's room, Killari asked her brother for news from Cusco.

- The majority of our families have been killed, or they have run away, leaving behind all their belongings. We know that Tamaya is preparing a marriage for Tinkupuma in Cusco. He will marry our cousin Kori, the beautiful daughter of Pushaq, our uncle. I have to confess to you that I had my own intentions of marrying her. Tamaya wants to join her bloodline with ours to validate the Emperor's authority and earn the respect of all the coastal chiefs. The wedding will take place this week. As a matter of fact, the festivities for the royal wedding have already begun. Within a few months it will be *Inti Raymi*, and Tinkupuma is considering throwing an unforgettable party. Many of our men will be present so that they can report the news of the big event to us. I would like to know how Kori is feeling about her wedding.

- We'll have to do something. We'll think of some plan of action without letting our mother know.

Chapter 14

The City of Cusco was alive with an unfettered rhythm of people coming and going, leaving offerings and gifts for the royal couple. Within a few days, the royal wedding would take place. The jewelers remained at their work benches, as they created new jewelry for the young Emperor and his future wife. Tamaya had an important role in the wedding and had also requested special jewelry for the occasion. Seamstresses, who were *mamacunas*, the oldest of the Sun Virgins, possessed the best fabrics of the Empire and selected the most magnificent for the royal family. Musicians and dancers created a unique performance for them. Cooks prepared the best sauces incorporating Andean aji chile peppers for a great variety of vegetables and grains, including corn, potato, sweet potato, yuca, quinoa, and bread made of *kiwicha*, a nutritious seed. They also prepared platters of Andean deer, sea lion, and fish from Lake Titicaca and the coastal waters. It was taken for granted that the celebration would provide an abundance of drinks and exotic fruits, such as *aguaymanto* (similar to a tomato in texture but with a sharp, sweet flavor), guavas, and *chirimoyas*.

The High Priest gave instructions to the maidens selected to help him during the wedding ceremony. The coastal chiefs sent precious cloths made of fine cotton in an assortment of colors and patterns, and other villages created ceramics especially for the occasion; strings of coca leaves were brought to the Royal Palace on the backs of llamas, for specific use in the ceremony led by the High Priest. The Emperor's vestment was created by a select group of Sun Virgins in *Acllahuasi,* the cloistered place where they lived. The cape was made of black vicuña fleece, indicating that Tinkupuma was in mourning for his father, but it was adorned with gold stitching and precious gems. All of the Emperor's ceremonial clothing could only be worn once, and then had to be burned.

Kori had lost a great deal of weight due to the stress under which her entire family lived. Nevertheless, her beauty was even more pronounced than usual, and all her clothing, which had to be tailored on her multiple times a day, ultimately fit her perfectly. In advance of her mother's approval, four women hairstylists experimented with numerous styles of braidings and hair arrangements for the bride's nuptials. The chosen style must be beautiful, but more modest than the Emperor's, being neither more important nor bigger than his.

Finally, the long-awaited day for the royal wedding arrived.

Several attendants in service to Tinkupuma dressed him for the occasion. After bathing and massaging him with floral essential oils, they dressed him in his royal gown made of *qunpi*[11], the finest material woven in the Acllahuasi. It was embellished with golden shoulder pads and bracelets. The earrings, crafted of gold, reached down to his shoulders. Tinkupuma also had a jeweler create the *llawt'u*, a headdress constructed of tiny hairs of the vampire bat. His shoes were of leather and animal skins.

The most important item was the *Mascaipacha*, more commonly known as the Emperor's crown. It was a rope woven of thirty-two strings that was then wrapped around the Emperor's head. It consisted of a tassel of red fiber with incrustations of golden strings and feathers from the *corequenque*[12], an Andean bird of great religious symbolism. His coat was made of vicuña fiber studded with jewels and turquoise stones. He was now dressed as *Intiq Churin,* a semi-divine man, the Son of the Sun.

Three women from Kori's family braided her hair into very small plaits so that her royal diadem would fit well. They placed the royal head-covering called *sukupa* on her head, fastening it with a gold clip. The earrings were priceless pendants of gold embedded with

---

[11] Qunpi - Wool made from the vicuña, used in royal fabrics.
[12] Corequenque - Mountain caracara bird.

precious stones, and she wore bracelets appropriate to her social rank. Her dress, or tunic, was white, made of the best cotton brought from the northern coast. The brightly-colored hem was finished in geometric patterns. Kori's shawl made of vicuña fleece was very light and covered her shoulders. It was fastened with a gold *tupu* or brooch, shaped like a turquoise hummingbird head. The waist of her garment was held together by a *tocapo*[13] as a special adornment for the dress. Her small bouquet was a collection of wildflowers, prepared by her most loyal servants. Kori was gorgeous, but she bore a sadness and distress because she would have far preferred to marry Unay, who had been her companion since they were very young, and of whom she had beautiful memories. She knew her great love had run away from a certain death at the hands of Tinkupuma.

Tamaya wanted to be the most beautiful and admired woman at the wedding ceremony. It was not difficult for her to achieve it. Her Quito-style hair would attract lots of attention and her jewels brought from Quito would cause everyone to fixate on them. Her entire outfit was spectacular, with precious emeralds and pearls sewn onto her long cape. Her desire was for everyone to appreciate her as the *Coya* of the Empire—the most important woman after the Emperor. Her headdress incorporated unique feathers, native to the eastern edge of the Empire, and never before seen in the region of Cusco

Tamaya said to her servant,

- Tell me, how do I look?

- Like the most beautiful woman in the Tahuantinsuyo, my lady.

- I want you to be more specific. Give me details.

- I have never seen more beautiful skin. Every aspect about you has perfect balance. Your hair is so black and shiny, it has a bluish tint. Your body is so well-proportioned that all

---

[13] Tocapo - A set of colorful squares with geometric decoration.

people constantly admire it. You are like an Inca goddess. Everything about the way you look is sublime.

- Give me the silver-plated mirror so I can see myself again. Continue preparing me, so that everyone can see me as the most beautiful woman in all the land.

Kori's mother dressed in an elegant way for her social position, but she was also simple. Her preference was to avoid attracting attention. She had heard about Tamaya's personality and advised her husband to follow her own example. He agreed.

The day began with a fog having over the city, followed by a strong sun. The Emperor asked the High Priest if this was a good omen. The High Priest said:

- The fog heralds pure air and is a good sign. The wedding ceremony will be grand, and you will receive your people's blessing. We have burned coca leaves in the Temple of Coricancha as well as in the Temple of the Moon Goddess. Everyone hopes you will produce a great number of descendants, my lord. We will have the fertility ceremonies in the fields of the Sacred Valley.

Everything was ready for the elaborate ceremony in the City of Cusco.

The High Priest headed the parade riding in the Royal palanquin carried by several men. The bride followed him, carried in a similar fashion, until they got to the Temple. Only royal families and close servants attended the ceremony. A great many soldiers encircled the Temple. After the ceremony in the Temple, they moved to the Royal Palace where the couple partook of a specially prepared dish of llama meat. The couple remained chaste during the four days of the celebration, which culminated in the consummation of their marriage.

Kori was very nervous that night. She wanted to disappear just as Unay, and his mother and sister had. She asked the Moon Goddess to protect her as she did not want to bear Tinkupuma's children. When he appeared in the royal bedroom ready to sleep with his wife. Kori closed her eyes, fantasizing it was Unay to whom she was giving herself instead.

Chapter 15

Machu Picchu awoke with a heavy fog hanging over the city, so that Huayna Picchu's form was barely visible through the mist. Three *chasquis* arrived with news from Cusco. Unay received them, anxious to know what noteworthy information they brought. The news was of the marriage of Tinkupuma and Kori and the ongoing celebration of their wedding in the City. They reported that people admired Tamaya's great beauty, but many also complimented the bride's appearance. However, they continued, many observed a great sadness in Kori. At no time did they ever observe a smile on her face. Unay realized why she appeared sad. Surely, she was thinking of him. The chasquis observed that she must have considered planning an escape but decided it would have been too risky.

The other news came from the north of the Tahuantinsuyo. Foreigners had been sighted by the communities in that region. They were different, white-skinned, with long cottons on their faces. Their bodies were covered with a metal shell. But the most unsettling concern was the monstrous animals they had, which appeared to be half-man and half-beast. The men rode on top of these animals which were totally unknown to the Incas, being a true monument of muscles with a braided tail. Their power was immense, and their speed had never been witnessed. Moreover, these foreigners had deadly weapons that spewed fire, and they carried swords and lances that they used adeptly. Unay received these reports from the *chasqui*s. They told him that Tinkupuma was aware of these events and that he had sent many spies to observe them and report back to him. To demonstrate his great power to the foreigners, Tinkupuma planned first, to find Unay, as a confirmation of the Empire's unity under a single Emperor. His intention was to indicate there were no signs of division or weakness on the part of the reigning Inca Ruler.

The white men resembled the god Viracocha, and for the time being, the native Andean people considered them to be gods who were previously unknown to them, and who possessed magical powers. These foreigners had already provided themselves with native informants who wanted to help because they were opposed to the reigning Emperor, who had decimated their population with the use of his army. Among the informants was Felipe. The white-skinned foreigners were Spanish and called him Felipillo because he had been with them since he was very young. He spoke both Quechua and Spanish and served as their interpreter, frequently rescuing the white men from a lot of trouble.

Chapter 16

In the Imperial Palace of Cusco, Kori summoned her nursemaid, Llacsa, requesting that she permanently stay in the palace with her because she would not accept any other lady-in-waiting. Kori opened her heart up to Llacsa and told her that she was very unhappy as Tinkupuma's wife. She loved Unay and she did not want to have her husband's children.

- You have knowledge of so many herbs, and their properties both good and bad, as well as their antidotes.

- Yes, My Lady. You are right. What is it that you want?

- For you to give me the particular herbs to prevent me from bearing my husband's children.

- If this is discovered, they will torture and kill me, and my family as well.

- Nobody will find out, because I will drink your brews in private.

- I will have to ask my ancestors' permission in a secret ceremony.

- You have to hurry, Llacsa. If I conceive his child, it will be too late.

- You will have your answer tomorrow.

The next day Llacsa delivered the herbs in a cotton sack. She instructed Kori in their preparation and use and stressed the importance of her being alone when she drank the preparation. And so, it was.

Several months passed and Tinkupuma's mother asked why her daughter-in-law was not yet with child. She called for her.

- Kori, I have requested your presence to find out how you are.

- I am fine. Thank you for asking.

- They tell me that you have yet to conceive a child. What is the problem?

- Nothing outside of the normal. I know that that my mother waited for two years before she was with child. It's likely that I am like her.

- You are going to have to hurry up. The Empire needs descendants immediately.

- I will do what is necessary, *Coya*. You do not need to worry.

- I hope to hear some news soon.

- So it shall be.

Kori returned to the palace very worried. There was no way of talking to her cousins Unay and Killari. There was no way of finding them. Until one day her nursemaid spoke to her:

- I have heard from your cousins.

- What do you mean? asked Kori nervously.

- Your cousin Unay has agents planted in the palace. He wants to know if you are happy.

- You can tell him that I am not.

- I have to be thoughtful, deciding whether someone is a spy or is simply working for your mother-in-law.

- That is true. I hope we are lucky.

- I will have to give them an answer today.

- Keep me updated. It is extremely important for me.

Chapter 17

The month of June arrived, when the Festival of *Inti Raymi was* observed both in Cusco and Machu Picchu. It celebrated the winter solstice, the beginning of the harvest season. The Emperor presided over the festivities along with his generals, princes, and governors. They all gathered at dawn, dressed in their finest garments, and carrying their respective shields and scepters.

A procession prepared to approach the *Coricancha* before the sun rose. It was led by Tinkupuma, his wife Kori, and the royal family, with Tamaya in a prominent position, as well as the High Priest and the musicians.

The Emperor was seated on a golden palanquin, dressed in fine clothing, wearing a necklace of emeralds, and gold earrings with precious stones representing the sun and the moon.

The musicians played sorrowful music to express the absence of the Sun God, *Inti*. At the precise moment the sun appeared through the skies, the music became joyful and Tinkupuma greeted the *Inti*. The warriors and people all shouted out joyfully, and the High Priest offered *aqha*[14], the traditional drink of the Sun God.

Mummies of the former Inca emperors, housed in the Temple, were displayed. The noble families also participated in the festivities, richly dressed for the occasion. The ceremony lasted all day until Tinkupuma, Kori, and the entire royal family returned to the palace to rest. The mummies were then returned to the Temple

---

[14] Aqha - A beverage from fermented corn, chicha.

of the Sun by the nobles devoted to protecting them; it was a great honor for them to carry out this duty.

Chapter 18

After Unay received the response to his question regarding Kori's feeling about her marriage, he met with his mother and Killari.

- Kori is very unhappy, and she would escape tomorrow if she could. I must figure out the perfect strategy for her to break free. The palace's security is practically impregnable, with guards everywhere. The only possibility would be for Kori to leave the palace under the guise of visiting her family. The only problem with that, is her parents could be accused of involvement, even though they know nothing about the plan. Unfortunately, they just might have to pay for it, but it is a risk I will have to take. Kori cannot stay in Cusco any longer.

- Anku can help you. He did an excellent job with my escape from the palace. He would have to disguise himself so that no one would recognize him, said Killari.

- The plan has to be faultless. We can't risk losing Anku, insisted Rahua Ocllo, their mother.

- As soon as I have everything in place, I will let you know what I have decided.

Kori learned through Llacsa that Unay had a plan to bring her to his hiding place. She had no other information except that she was to schedule a visit to her parents' house, as she normally did once a week, and then return home after dinner. She was to wear the same royal clothing as was her custom. Kori did as she was instructed. The night of the visit she noticed a man and two women crossing her path as she was returning to the palace. They grabbed her and took her to a pitch-black location, instructing her to exchange clothing with one of the women. The man informed her that they had come on behalf of Unay and that they would take her to him. The girl who traded her humble dress for the royal gown knew that she was risking her own life.

Anku left immediately with Kori for the outskirts of the Imperial City. They waited until the woman who had exchanged clothing with Kori returned, and then they left, joined by Llacsa.

The next day, the alarm went out. Kori had disappeared along with her nursemaid Llacsa. They looked everywhere but they could not find any clue about the women's whereabouts. The last time they had seen Kori was when she returned to the palace and went into her bedroom. The next day she was no longer there.

Anku planned for them to travel by a secret road, but still they took all the necessary precautions. In a week they reached the Hidden City.

Kori thought she was living a dream. Killari and her mother welcomed her.

- Welcome, cousin Kori, said Killari, embracing her.

- You can feel at home here, said her aunt, Killari's mother.

- Thank you for saving me from an unhappy life with Tinkupuma.

- We learned from my brother that you wanted to escape from Cusco.

- Where is he? asked Kori, hiding a smile.

- He's on his way. He's very excited to see you. We will leave you two alone to talk privately.

- Thank you. We have a lot to say.

Unay arrived alone. He was ecstatic when he saw Kori, yet he didn't say a word.

- Unay, I've missed you so much!

- So, have I, Kori.

- It seems like a dream, being here with you, far away from the nightmare of Tinkupuma.

- I understand, yet you look beautiful, even more than before.

- I have come here to be with you. I've left everything, my family and my position in society, but it doesn't matter to me. It's a relief to be here with you, safe.

- We will protect you here. You will be my wife, my heart's desire. The wedding ceremony will be tomorrow.

- Hold me, Unay. Tell me you will love me forever.

- That is my promise to you.

Chapter 19

Tinkupuma arrived at the palace in a furious state. He had traveled from Quito having achieved various conquests in the north of the Empire, which filled him with joy and delight.

Nevertheless, the news that came from Cusco made him crazed. He could not believe that his wife, Kori, had disappeared without leaving a trace. Because he knew the security in the Imperial Palace of Cusco had never been exemplary, he decided to return to Cusco on the most direct route possible. He reached the city that very night and spoke with his mother, the *Coya* Tamaya.

- Mother, what you are telling me is crazy! We had agreed that my wife would have the utmost security.

- She did, but she was taken as she was leaving her own house, where the security guards felt there was a safe environment.

- Have they interrogated any suspects?

- They have already been threatened under penalty of death, but we have not gotten anything out of them.

- In Quito I took two concubines. One of them is pregnant, so in five months you will be a grandmother.

- Thank you, son, that is excellent news.

- We have to keep looking for Kori and offer a generous reward for anyone who knows anything about this affair.

- Our generals are already taking care of it.

- Tomorrow I want you to choose two concubines to calm me after this long journey.

Chapter 20

All of Machu Picchu was in a festive and joyful mood, for the Emperor Unay was to marry Kori that very day. Killari and her mother spent the day preparing for the ceremony, and the *mamacunas* busied themselves dressing the bride. As was the custom, Unay received massages and baths before being dressed. The ceremony was planned for noon, when the sun would be at the height of its splendor in the Temple of the Sun. The High Priest had carefully prepared the religious rite so that the royal family would be pleased with the service. Kori arrived, along with ten *mamacunas,* as well as Killari and her mother. Unay was already at the Temple and awaited Kori beside the High Priest. Unay's masculine beauty was conspicuous and the joy displayed on his face made him all the more handsome.

Killari was saddened knowing that Anku would not be at the wedding because of his guard duties that day. The wedding ceremony was short, but the celebration that followed lasted the traditional four days, and included huge platters of food, and musicians who enlivened the party. The wedding day was filled with peace and happiness.

Despite Kori's joy, she remained stressed, having left her family behind, not knowing what might happen to them.

She addressed the problem with Unay,

- Dear husband, I would like to know what is happening with my family, as I fear that Tinkupuma and above all, his mother, might have taken their revenge on my parents.

- I will send my men to find out.

- Thank you, Unay. I can't sleep thinking about what might have happened to them in my absence.

In a few days the couple received news of Kori's family. Her parents had been forced to abandon their house on Tamaya's orders. They became exiles and pariahs in the Empire of the four *suyos,* as nobody was allowed to shelter or help them. They had traveled to the north of the City of Cusco with some staff who had loyally served in their household for many years. However, it was not difficult to find them. Anku and General Kallpa were charged with secretly bringing them to the Hidden City. A few days later they arrived in Machu Picchu and were stunned to find their beloved daughter, Kori there. They were fully aware of why she had left her husband Tinkupuma, but now she was happily the wife of her beloved Unay, the man she had always loved.

Chapter 21

In Cusco, Tinkupuma met with his generals. The situation was urgent, and they needed to make a decision. The bearded white foreigners who resembled Viracocha had been seen in Tumbes and were on their way to Cajamarca.

- I prohibit the comparison of these new arrivals with our God, Viracocha. They are nothing more than humans, and there is no reason to be afraid of them, the Emperor said.

- They have come with two kinds of monsters. One has four legs and a long tail and is very fast. The other one spews fire from its mouth and can kill many men with a single blast, said one of the generals.

- We need to observe them until we find their weakness. There are only a few of them, and so many of us. For now, we have to focus our energy on defeating my brother, Unay. He does not acknowledge me as the Emperor, and I know that he is arming himself to begin a war. A conflict between brothers is not in our best interest. We would just be providing the foreigners greater reason to invade, and they would take advantage of the timing to attack us more easily.

- What worries me the most is not the war, sir, but the sickness that is decimating the Empire's population. It is a pustulous outbreak of the skin that kills people by the thousands. *Chay mana allin chas'ka onqochisunqui,* —that bad star will make you ill—said the priest. In the Andes it is called *huchuy muru oncoy,* and it is a deadly disease.

People are saying that it was this sickness that killed the late Emperor, your father.

- We have never seen this sickness before in the Tahuantinsuyo. Where does it come from? asked the young Emperor.

- I have sacrificed animals, and in their entrails, I have seen the answer. It was these foreigners—the bearded white men have brought it, and the gods say that these men will bring even more diseases never before seen in this land. These are their most effective weapons against us, the people of the ancient mountains.

- You are right, High Priest. We must fight against these new diseases with our age-old knowledge, said Tinkupuma. The enemy is in the north. I must go there and observe them. For the time being, we must find Unay and take him prisoner. We have concluded that war against my brother is the only solution to consolidate the Empire. Afterward, we will decide how to eliminate the foreigners.

- Your wish is our command. We are ready to die for our Emperor, sir, aid the General

- Tomorrow, we will begin an expedition in search of Unay.

Tinkupuma ended the meeting with these words,

- You, my generals, Rumiñahui, Quizquiz, Calicuchima, bring forth proposals to commence a war with my brother.

Chapter 22

Killari had not seen Anku for several weeks, and she missed him desperately. She sent for him.

- Anku, I have been told that you are preparing for war with Tinkupuma, which I see, takes up all your time.

- Yes, it is true, Princess.

- I think we should talk about our feelings.

- Princess Killari, I feel incapable of telling you anything about my feelings. I am a humble man.

- I understand, so I will be the one to speak first. My feelings for you are deep and noble. My father promised me a man of the nobility, but I never accepted his plan. The nobleman's name is Suri, and our relationship will never lead to marriage. My mother already knows how I feel about you. Therefore, you must speak honestly with me.

- You know that I care for you more than anyone. I would give my life to protect you.

- Would you marry me?

- That is a dream; it can never happen. You are the *ñusta* of the Empire, the Inca Princess.

- If you want it to be, it's possible. My mother has already given her consent, and she has spoken with Unay. He has also consented.

- …

- Anku, say something. You've gone silent! Say something!

- I don't know what to say. I think I'm either going crazy or I'm dreaming!

- I thought this moment would be more romantic.

- Don't go anywhere, Princess. I'll be right back.

Anku disappeared and returned after half an hour. He brought with him the most magnificent orchid that he had in his garden.

- This is my gift for the best and most beautiful flower in the Empire of four *suyos*

- It's an exceptional specimen of an orchid. Thank you, Anku.

- I don't have any riches to offer you, but my love is immense, and I will demonstrate it to you every day until I take my last breath.

- Come closer, Anku, and hold me.

The couple kissed for a long time, and they sat together gazing at the setting of the sun, a truly spectacular sight from where they were in Machu Picchu. Killari's pets approached, Puquy the pretty white alpaca, Kusi the black dog, and Rumi the black jaguar of the jungle. A little farther off, the two children from the jungle played. Everything was balanced and perfect, in a world of peace and harmony. Killari's dream was becoming reality. The gods, nature, and humanity were in perfect communion.

Chapter 23

Killari and Anku's wedding ceremony was one of the premier celebrations of the year. They were both happy and beautiful. Killari's mother and the Emperor Unay, with his wife Kori, presided over the festivities. The High Priest married them, sacrificing a white llama as tradition required. Food was prepared for the guests with the blood of the llama. Musicians entertained and Anku played his *quena*, the Andean flute. More than a hundred musicians participated, with all kinds of instruments, including percussions, *quenas*, and *zampoñas*[15]. The festivities lasted four days.

In the intimacy of their room, Killari and Anku loved one another intensely. In a moment of passion, Killari said slowly to her beloved:

- <<Find me in the coastal dunes, so close to Caral[16],
  Follow me to the heights of Misti to see the condors
  Cross the abyss of Colca.

  Row, row with me on the river of our inner jungle;
  unearth the undiscovered outposts in your path;
  enrapture yourself inside the squared sun,
  framed by your moonlit beach,
  Follow me to the steps of Machu Picchu,
  until we find ourselves in front of Intihuatana
  in a ritual rendezvous to admire Huayna Picchu.

  What dawns will wake us up to paint them!
  What twilights will await us to whisper to them!>>

Anku looked at her in ecstasy.

---

[15] Zampoñas - Traditional Andean panpipes.
[16] Caral - A large settlement in the Supe Valley, north of Lima. It is the most ancient city of the Americas and a well-studied site.

- I will put music to your words, my darling Princess. I will always follow you wherever you go. I will be your shadow, your torch, your guiding star. I will always love you and protect you. Now listen to what I have to say to you:

«Your gaze, dark,
of great mystery,
unfathomable in its
profundity.

This opening,
immeasurable
in your fixed gaze,
penetrating,
that calls to the
ancient search,
to the primitive disguise,
to the essence
of being.

It is the silent call,
the magnetic approach,
chemical attraction
of spirits made
real.

How much we say when we see one another!
How much we see when we speak to one another!

And I...
get lost
sweetly
in this gloomy woodland,
crystalline,
wandering timelessly
into the depth of your eyes.

They fell asleep nestled together, happy in the knowledge of their mutual love, and having promised eternal love to each other. They had traveled side-by-side through much of the Tahuantinsuyo without becoming bored with each other, secretly loving one another.

At the end of the festivities, Kori called for her husband.

- What do you desire, my beloved Kori?

- I want to give you some news that makes me very happy. Six months have passed since we were married. I have been taking herbs to grow stronger. And they have produced very good results.

- Yes, you look beautiful.

- I have your child inside of me. And many weeks have passed, and I have not menstruated. Within six months we will be parents.

- Kori, this news fills me with joy! It is an excellent omen, especially now that we are getting ready to defeat Tinkupuma.

- You have to promise me that you will not go to war. Send your generals. They will know how to direct our soldiers.

- I can neither lie to you, nor please you. The battle will begin in two months. I must go with my men, but I promise you that I will take care of myself. Does my mother already know the news of your being with child?

- No, but I believe she senses it.

- We will go together to tell her the good news.

Unay's mother received the news excitedly. From that moment, her health improved noticeably. In fact, she seemed younger.

In just a few months, the heir to the Empire of the Incas of the Cusco Hanan royal family would be born, and would be named Sayri Túpac, son of Unay and his *coya*, Kori.

Chapter 24

The war between the two brothers was not only long, it was the bloodiest confrontation in the history of the Inca Empire. The two factions were very strong, and their generals constantly evaluated new military strategies to attain victory. Neither one was willing to concede, while the male populations were noticeably decreasing. The white men were referred to as *viracochas*, because they were white, and they came from the sea like the Andean Creator of the Universe called Viracocha. When these foreigners learned of the war between the two brothers, they knew it would be advantageous for them, assessing that they eventually would likely be victorious over the native people. The greatest causes of death, however, were two illnesses never before seen in the Empire. The symptoms of one included extreme nasal congestion accompanied by a cough and high fever, which the white men called the grip or influenza. The other produced large skin welts and a substantial fever. It was truly an epidemic, since it obviously spread very rapidly. Children and elders quickly succumbed. The healers in the north observed that the white men did not fall ill, which made them suspect that these men were protected by supernatural forces. They burned coca leaves to ask the gods to cleanse them and protect them from all the evils brought by the destroyers of the Empire. Since the dead could not be cremated due to religious prohibition, the sicknesses spread easily throughout the land.

Tinkupuma opted to journey to Cajamarca to see the foreigners with his own eyes. He made that decision after a heated discussion with his generals. They were desperate to make those seemingly few white men disappear because they counted themselves in the thousands. Tinkupuma had rejected their decision to confront the white men because he considered them harmless. It would be easy to do away with them because there were so few, however he was also not familiar with the proverb that says, «There is no such thing as a small enemy.» His generals wanted to decimate the foreigners, so they could freely dedicate themselves to fighting Unay's armies. Moreover, many people were helping the white enemy in resisting the Inca rule. At last, the Emperor complied with his generals' insistence, and agreed to face these people who were erroneously referred to as *viracochas*.

Tinkupuma approached the City of Cajamarca with thousands of warriors ready to die for him. They carried him in a royal palanquin with hundreds of unarmed warriors surrounding the Emperor as protection. When Tinkupuma entered Cajamarca, he was preceded by dozens of servants using brooms, sweeping the path clean, ahead of their master's arrival.

The white men, mounted upon their horses, were prepared to charge at them, and they did so. They shouted, «Santiago, Santiago!» and then their horses lunged forward, with the bells that adorned them clanging noisily. They advanced, wielding their lances and killed many of the Emperor's warriors. Finally, after killing everyone who preceded and shielded the Emperor, the leader of the white men captured Tinkupuma. He grabbed the Emperor by his long hair and threw him to the ground. Contrary to the custom of Inca rulers, Tinkupuma wore his hair long to hide the missing ear that he had lost earlier during the wars of conquest in the Empire's northern territory. Seeing their king captive, the warriors fled, terrified.

General Rumiñahui resolved to go to Quito to recruit more soldiers and then return to Cajamarca. In truth, he planned to conquer Quito and revolt against Tinkupuma, and that is what he did. He ordered the killing of the two warring brothers and their relatives so that he could usurp all the power in the region.

Chapter 25

Unay discovered that Tinkupuma was being held captive, and that his people were gathering gold and silver to pay ransom to the white men for him. Unay decided that this was the right time to come out of hiding and return to Cusco to take control of the Empire as reigning Emperor. He requested to see both his mother and sister.

- Tinkupuma has been captured in the north of the Empire, in the city of Cajamarca. It is a convenient time for me to go to Cusco and present myself to the people as their legitimate ruler.

- A large part of his army is still in Cusco, brother. Do not risk yourself. You must be very cautious. Tinkupuma is as sly as a fox.

- Your sister is right, his mother said. Besides, you have to make sure to protect your son and your wife Kori, who is expecting another child.

- This is not the right time to leave, Unay. We have to think of a strategy to protect ourselves. Your life is very important to us and we cannot lose you. I am going to discuss this with Anku to see what he can suggest.

- We have to make a decision soon. The Empire cannot go on without a leader. It would be a huge error if the chiefs thought there was no Emperor to govern them, and they rebelled against us and helped the white invader, worried Unay.

- Yes, you're right, son, said his mother.

Killari related her conversation with Unay to Anku and asked him what advice he could offer.

- It is very important to not put the Emperor at risk. We have to contrive some scheme of someone impersonating him, someone disguised as Unay, and looks enough like him, so that people who know him will think that the man is your brother. Only a few generals will know the truth. Later he can go to Cusco when things calm down and we can see more clearly what has to be done with the *viracochas* who have invaded. They say that there are only a few of them, but Tinkupuma's men think that they are the sons of Viracocha and messengers of Pachacamac[17]. Tinkupuma himself acknowledged this subsequent to his original disbelief and demanded that his men treat them like gods. People say that Tinkupuma believes that the prophecy of Pachacamac priests is coming true. That the *viracochas* will come from the sea to take control of the Tahuantinsuyo, Anku said, upset.

- It seems wise to protect my brother. Your plan of replacing him seems excellent. We will have to work very carefully to select the right one to impersonate him. It must be someone we can trust completely. Let's visit with my brother to inform him of your plan.

Unay accepted Anku's strategy and congratulated him on the flawlessness of the details.

In addition, Unay's men brought important news. The white men were on their way to Pachacamac, the ancient coastal Sanctuary, to take all the objects of gold and silver that were there. This was to be part of the ransom for Tinkupuma. It would be necessary to protect the idol that was in the Sanctuary. The best thing to do would be to remove it from the Temple and hide it in a sacred burial place, a *huaca*. Unay ordered Anku to take charge of this mission.

---

[17] Pachacamac - The Inca God of Fire.

Anku accepted, and then spoke with Killari about the mission with which Unay had entrusted him.

- I will have to leave tonight, toward the coast, with a few men to accompany me.

- I will go with you. This mission appeals to me since I have never gone to the coast and I have never seen the sea.

- Right now, the Empire is in chaos. I do not want you to put yourself at risk. Besides, your brother would not agree to it.

- I will go see him, said Killari, resolved to convince him.

Unay was with Kori, who had just given birth. The couple was quite happy as they now had two children. The second baby was a girl.

- Sweet family, it gives me great pleasure to see you all so happy. I've come to ask a big favor of Unay. I want to go with my husband on the mission you have given to him.

- It is very dangerous for you to leave, now that the Empire's situation is so uncertain.

- I have felt a strong calling by the gods to save the idol of Pachacamac. I must hide it in a burial mound, a huaca, that only I know. It is in Arequipa, between the Misti and the Chachani volcanoes. I intend to hold a ceremony there and pray to our gods to protect us from the invasion of the white men, and to keep Tinkupuma from finding us. I will also plead for them to determine our destiny.

- I feel uneasy knowing that you are risking your life with this task.

- Wherever Anku goes, I will go. Now let me speak with the High Priest so that he can teach me the steps of the ceremony that I will perform when I get to the main *huaca* in Arequipa.

- May the gods be with you, my dear sister.

- Do not take a risk by leaving Machu Picchu. We need you, said Killari.

Chapter 26

Killari and Anku departed, dressed in simple peasant clothing. It was important that they not be recognized by anyone; they had to be painstakingly cautious. For safety reasons they traveled by night despite the dangers they might face. The group of travelers consisted of five people, and they had three llamas to bear the heavy weight of the packs. Their provisions contained nothing of great value, but only practical objects for cooking, sleeping, and protecting themselves from the elements. They traveled by the Road System of the Tahuantinsuyo known as Quapaq Ñan[18], toward Vilcas Huaman, and later northward to Jauja. From there they headed down to the coast toward Pachacamac. Anku was quite familiar with the road because his family had lived in Jauja and he had gone to the coast many times with them. Later, his family relocated to the Sacred Valley.

The group safely reached the Sanctuary of Pachacamac. Upon arriving, they noticed that the holy place had not yet been desecrated. At the top of the temple, they spied a golden statue of a fox. The idol of Pachacamac, which was kept in a dark cave, had to be removed immediately, and replaced with another similar object, for the white men would not know the difference. The idol was made of wood, which was noteworthy since it would have no perceived value to the infidels who came from the sea. The heavy, tall idol was covered with a textile in preparation for transporting to the holy burial site, the Sacred Huaca in Arequipa. Killari was so

---

[18] Quapaq Ñan - An extensive and advanced Inca road network and transportation system. It covered the length and breadth of the Andes and took several centuries to build. The network, emanating from the center of Cusco, had four main routes and many branches.

worried about preserving the idol as best she could, that she forgot about one of her major objectives, going to the sea. Anku recognized his wife's weighty concern, so he embraced her and whispered in her ear.

- Tonight, we will travel to the sea and sleep there. I want you to arise with the Spring sun and see the beauty of our sea. The dunes of this place have a great natural beauty. You will swim alongside me in the blue waters of the salty ocean; we will dine on seafood and walk barefoot along the endless beach. It will be your first adventure in the coastal waters of the Empire. I want to see you happy. I want you to smile at our future, because we will survive the war, the death, and the sicknesses that are punishing the Empire of the Tahuantinsuyo.

- <<Thank you, Anku. I needed you to cheer me. Afterwards we will begin the journey to Arequipa to finish our mission. When we arrive, I will have to specifically follow the ceremony of exaltation and enthronement of the idol of Pachacamac into the Sacred Huaca. At that point I will feel more at peace.

- Everything will fall into place just as the gods have designed. We are obeying the will of the Oracle.

- It will be my first deed as priestess of the Empire. We have to save our past and preserve our future.

They arrived at the dunes near the sea to spend the night, sleeping soundly until dawn. Anku was already awake when Killari opened her eyes.

- Where are we Anku? Killari asked, frightened.

- In the dunes, close to the sea. Get up. I want you to view the most wonderful spectacle you have ever seen.

They walked hand-in-hand and Killari saw the endless expanse of blue that lost itself on the horizon, and the sun that rose up victorious, in the east, to illuminate the surface of the ocean. She observed that the waters moved constantly and asked Anku about the frothy foam on the shore.

- It's the crashing waves that create this white foam. It warns us that the sea is alive, and we have to respect it. It gives us fish, every kind of seafood, and algae which is edible, too. They say that mankind came from the sea, just like our god Viracocha.

- Now that I have seen the sea I don't want to leave. It will be difficult to depart, knowing that a marvel as great as this exists.

- We will return, my beloved Princess. I promise.

They stayed for two days, enjoying the landscape Killari had never before witnessed. Then they packed all the necessities and planned the remainder of the journey. They traveled toward the south, skirting along the coastal road, passing through Inka Huasi, Puka Tampu, and Chala, until arriving at Atico, from which they would climb to Arequipa, at an altitude of about 2,300 meters (7,500 feet). Since they knew they would be walking for several days, they brought many changes of sandals for each of them, should they need them. The journey was arduous, but the effort to protect the idol of the Empire was worthwhile.

Chapter 27

They arrived in Arequipa exhausted, but pleased that the most difficult part of the journey was over. The next task was burying the idol of Pachacamac. They quickly found the road to the Sacred Huaca and managed to get to the site without any great difficulty. They began digging, and Killari prepared herself to begin the religious ceremony. She dressed in the special clothing the High Priest had supplied and uttered the words he taught her. The entire group assisted in moving the wooden idol and safely placing it again in an erect position, just as it had been in Pachacamac. They also left some specific objects and coca leaves in worship of the god, and to pray for his assistance in this mission. The entrance was then closed, and they departed the site peacefully.

Killari was happy because they could now return to Machu Picchu. They knew they would have to be especially cautious as they approached Cusco since uncertainty and tension permeated the entire Empire. The armies of both sides continued battling over the Empire. Killari, Anku and the rest of the group chose the road of Hatum Colla on the approach to Cusco. They heard that a major tragedy had occurred there. All of the *viracochas* had reached Cusco, where they seized all the gold and silver they could find, as they dismantled the Temples of the Sun and the Moon. The guardians of the Temples had removed all of the embalmed bodies of the Incas that had been there. The body of the last deceased Inca, the father of Unay and Killari, had already been hidden. They were told that their brother Tinkupuma now was a prisoner of the *viracochas*. There were events occurring that spoke for themselves. The Empire was crumbling. There was not a single leader who stood out; all that remained was an absence of power.

It was very dangerous, since all the chiefs might now rebel, creating a situation of total instability.

Killari said to Anku,

- FIrst we have another mission to complete, locating the sacred body of my father. We must find where he has been taken and transport him to Machu Picchu as soon as possible, before the *viracochas* find him and want to ransom him for more gold and silver. We must immediately return to Machu Picchu for reinforcements.

- You are right. We have met many people who have both transported the wounded and moved dead bodies for burial. The Empire is being destroyed bit by bit. The armies have destroyed fields and faced an endless war. I am not sure it is a good idea for your brother to be in Cusco, the birthplace of the world, as the only Emperor. The *viracochas* have an insatiable thirst for riches and they are not going to obey any Emperor. We must go to Machu Picchu to warn Unay. That decision is up to him. First, we will locate the body of your father, our beloved late Emperor, and we will take him to Machu Picchu where he will rest in peace forever. There we will express our love and respect for him.

- Thank you, Anku. I needed to hear your support. Let's take the road to Cusco.

Chapter 28

In Cusco, Tamaya had received the bad news about her beloved son Tinkupuma, who was imprisoned by the men from the north, and she began distrusting everyone around her. She perceived that they were all Unay's spies who wanted her dead. Fearing that she would be poisoned, she ordered several servants to taste her food before she would try any. Tamaya remained in the palace, under self- imprisonment. She sent for the clairvoyant shaman, Paqari, who was the most respected woman in the Sacred Valley. She arrived accompanied by three women and two men.

- Are you Paqari, the seer? Tamaya asked authoritatively.

- Yes, madam. That is why I have brought my animals and my assistants. I use these animals to foretell the future.

- Leave me alone with my guests, Tamaya ordered her servants.

- To see the future, I need only one very precise question. The answer will be given in the terms of the Oracle, and I will then have to interpret it. That is my work.

- My son Tinkupuma has been made a prisoner in Cajamarca, and I want to know if I will see him again and if he will be treated well, as his lineage deserves.

- I will burn llama fat and coca leaves to be able to answer that question, the sorceress said.

- Go on, Tamaya ordered.

As she carried out the ceremony, Paqari saw the outlines of the deities providing her with the keys to see the future. She closed her eyes, and when she reopened them, they were white, and she began to speak in a guttural voice, as if it were coming from a well.

- The god of the wind Huari, of the subterranean world of Urin Pacha, tells me that the spirits are angered by the feud between your son and his brother Unay. Evil winds are coming from the north, which bring mortal illness. The plague is invading us.

- Answer my question! interrupted the *coya,* Tamaya.

- The Hanan Pacha, the world above, tells me that you will see your son again. Therefore, you must travel to Quito as soon as possible, where you will meet your son. He is being treated as the Emperor, and his servants are taking care of him, but the bearded men have him imprisoned. Tinkupuma has ordered the death of his brother. This will bring him disgrace and If he is successful, Unay will die. In the Kay Pacha, the world of men, there will be great chaos if Unay is assassinated. You must prevent it, ensuring that his execution order is reversed, said Pagari.

- My servants will give you the agreed-on fee. You may go now, replies Tamaya.

- I have brought my *cuyes*, my guinea pigs, to take all evil and ills from you, and protect you from bad luck, insisted the shaman.

- That will not be necessary. My people will take care of it.

- As you wish, *Coya*, My Lady.

The meeting between Tamaya and the shaman ended there. Tamaya then gave orders for her to be brought directly to Quito. The next day, she embarked on the journey, accompanied by an important group of people close to her, and many soldiers.

Chapter 29

Anku and Killari rested in an area very near Cusco. They were in familiar territory and felt quite safe. The night temperature was cold, so they started a small bonfire to prepare their food and warm themselves. They were accompanied by several warriors and a few women who attended Killari. They never sensed that they were being spied upon, but, in fact, they were. The warriors who accompanied Tamaya had observed them, some of whom recognized Anku and the *ñusta*[19] Killari. They informed Tamaya, who then ordered them to capture Killari. She would be Tamaya's prize, and the *Coya* did not concern herself with respect to the fate of the others. If they did not apprehend Killari, the soldiers knew they would pay with their lives. The warriors had no problem subduing Killari, as they took her. Anku could do nothing since he had left to hunt for dinner, and when he returned, he was given the bad news. Anku could not believe what was happening. Killari and her warriors had disappeared completely, and it was impossible to find them.

- We have not yet arrived in Cusco to rescue the body of the Emperor, and now I find myself without my wife! We will have to reach Cusco first, rescue the body of our deceased Emperor, and then begin the journey to Machu Picchu. From there we will start the search for Killari, said Anku, his voice broken by sobs.

Killari was brought before Tamaya, her step-mother. The kidnappers had chained her and placed a bag over her head so

---

[19] Ñusta - Quechua word for Princess of the Empire.

she would not know where she was. She was in Quito, but she had no idea.

- Remove the bag from her, immediately! ordered Tamaya, yelling.

- You must be Tamaya, Tinkupuma's mother, said Killari calmly.

- You guessed right. You must have already heard of my legendary beauty. The same cannot be said about you.

- I have never entertained the thought of competing with anyone in terms of beauty. I prefer to be admired for my other qualities.

- Now, you can tell me where you have been. You and your mother disappeared on the same day, before we arrived in Cusco. What were you afraid of?

- It was more caution than fear, Tamaya.

- Well, go on and tell me: Where have you been?

- In the Sacred Valley, living like two peasants in the *ayllu* of one of my servants.

- Nobody believes that. You are going to have to give me precise information about where you have been. Surely with Unay. If you do not talk, I will leave you without food or water. Then we will torture you until you decide to tell me everything you know.

- You cannot torture me. Royal law forbids it.

- We are at war, my dear Killari. And during wartime, anything is possible.

- I do not have anything to say. You are wasting your time.

- We will see about that, after you have experienced the torture that my soldiers inflict.

Killari was brought to a cave. They left her there without food, tied tightly with ropes, and her ankles were shackled with chains that wounded her. She fell asleep. In her dreams, her father appeared. He gazed at her, sad and worried, approaching ever more closely, and cradled her in his arms.

- Killari, daughter of my soul, you must be strong. I will never abandon you. It was wrong of me to name Tinkupuma the reigning Emperor. I should have left him in Quito with his mother. You have to survive this test in order to help Unay and his family. I promise you that I will be by your side the entire time. Do not speak; just remain silent and pretend to have fainted. Do not accept any food or drink because they will want to give you herbs that will make you talk. I will always love you and protect you.

Killari was tortured for many days. Still, she refused any food or drink. She was incessantly interrogated about Unay's whereabouts and refused to answer until she finally fainted. She remained so for several hours, without speaking. Tamaya's soldiers informed the *Coya* about Killari's condition.

- She must be faking it, Tamaya said, incredulously.

- No, My Lady. She is very ill. For days she has neither eaten nor taken anything to drink. She could die at any moment.

- I will notify my son Tinkupuma that I have his sister as a prisoner. Call for the *chasquis* so that they can take the message to the Emperor.

- Yes, *Coya*, we will do it immediately said the servants, calling the *chasquis*.

- Inform the Emperor I am following his orders and will remain in Quito until he is released. We have his sister, Killari, imprisoned, and are interrogating her so that she will give us information about Unay's location. The *chasquis* must go very quickly. I want his reply tomorrow.

- As you wish, *Coya*, they responded in unison.

The answer arrived two days later. Tamaya was furious. She did not care to hear the explanations of the recently arrived *chasqui* , but demanded to receive the message instantly.

- We spoke with two generals of the Emperor. They relayed our message to your son, our Lord Tinkupuma, who wants to see his sister and has asked that she be treated well. He does not want anyone to hurt her. He has ordered that she be released today and enjoy the protection of some warriors.

Tamaya summoned the person in charge of Killari's imprisonment.

- I hope the Princess is in good condition for a trip. She must leave immediately.

- She will not be able to go. She is very weak. If we move her, she will not last the night.

- Call for the shaman and order her to restore Killari immediately.

The shaman forced Killari to drink a special brew prepared from coca and other plants. She removed the chains and ropes that had immobilized her. Then she bathed and dressed her appropriately as a princess. Killari awakened and began asking questions.

- Where am I? she said weakly.

- You are in good hands, Princess Killari. I am healing you so that you might travel on the royal palanquin to Cajamarca, to meet up with your brother Tinkupuma. From now on you must only drink the brew that I have prepared for you. Later you can have small mouthfuls of quinoa and corn, followed by the fruits that I have supplied to your attendants. You will arrive healthy at your destination.

- Thank you, madam. Has your brew made me speak inappropriately?

- No. Absolutely not. You have been totally silent. You have not even complained about the lashes from the whip that are on your back. The wounds have been treated, but they will have to continue to be cleansed during the journey so that they do not become infected. Unfortunately, they will leave scars.

- I do not understand what Tinkupuma wants of me, though I am quite curious. I am not fearful of seeing him.

Killari traveled that very day. She did not notice Tamaya as she left, but when she glanced back to note where she had been, she saw Tamaya seated on a tall chair. Once again, Killari perceived the black and gray presence behind Tamaya, and recognized that it had always been accompanied by monstrous souls from the underworld. Killari again returned her gaze forward, sensing a strong shiver running down her back.

The journey from Quito to Cajamarca was long, but above all, it was difficult for Killari. She was very weak and the wounds on her back prevented her from sleeping or resting, even though she was being carried on the royal palanquin with every comfort. The attendants gave her *mate* tea to lessen the pain. She ate very little because she missed Anku. She did not know if he was alive, if something had happened to him, or if he was imprisoned by Tinkupuma's troops. They arrived in Cajamarca early in the morning.

Chapter 30

Anku arrived in the City of Cusco completely bewildered and depressed. He would neither eat nor sleep, thinking of Killari. The men who accompanied him were very concerned, as they had never before witnessed him like this.

- Anku, you have to do something. We have a very important mission, to recover the sacred body of our deceased Emperor. Unay, our leader, has already been advised of our arrival in Cusco, and the importance of sending reinforcements for our daring venture. Once in Machu Picchu, we will go in search for your wife.

- And perhaps by then it will be too late. I will have failed her, and I would never see her again. I love her so much and I need her to be able to breathe, eat, and live by her side...

- Do not lose hope, Anku, said his closest friend. You will not solve anything that way. Let peace enter your soul and let hope be reborn in your heart.

- Thank you, Sathiri. I needed to hear your words of encouragement. Let's go! We have to find our Emperor Unay's men, who are waiting for us in Cusco.

- It appears that the remains of our ancestors have been protected. We must find those of Unay's father, for our priests have hidden his body. I do not think it will be easy convincing them to bring the body to the Hidden City, but now that Tinkupuma is a prisoner, they will understand that if we transport the remains to Machu Picchu, the late Emperor will be reunited with his son, Unay.

- You are right. This is what I personally know of the High Priest. He will allow us to carry the sacred remains of our deceased Emperor, concluded Anku.

They continued their way toward the fortress of Sacsayhuaman.

Chapter 31

In Cajamarca, the warriors who transported Killari spoke with Tinkupuma's generals. They informed these men that they had brought the Emperor's ransom in gold and silver, but above all they brought Princess Killari, who, as ordered by the Emperor, had to meet with him upon arrival. General Rumiñahui was updated on all events. He then ordered his men to bring the gold and silver objects to where Tinkupuma was being held, and he also falsely reported to the foreigners that the wife of the Emperor had arrived to see him, believing that the bearded men would better understand the particular need for them to see each other. And so, it was. Killari was taken on the palanquin to Tinkupuma.

Killari entered the room and saw her brother seated on a chair that had been provided for the audience.

- Your body appears well-conditioned from hard work and exercise as I have been told that you climb mountains and commune with the condors. I want to speak with you, brother to sister. You must have already heard the news of my pending execution. I hope to convince them not to burn me as an infidel, as they refer to me, if I accept conversion to their religion and become baptized with names of their faith. In exchange I would accept death by garrotte[20], strangulation. Thus, my body would not be cremated, enabling my soul to live on in Uku Pacha, the world of the dead.

---

[20] Garrote - A wire, rope or other similar apparatus used for Strangulation.

- It is a pity to see you under these circumstances. Your ambition and arrogance have made you an unworthy leader of our Empire. You did not heed the words of our father, who will soon be resting in his rightful place. This war between you brothers has done nothing but weaken our Empire and strengthen the enemy. Could you not have been satisfied with the government of Quito, as our father had wished?

- It is not smart to have two leaders in an empire, as my mother always taught me; it is unprecedented. We should not turn ourselves into Sachamama, the serpent with two heads.

- How incredible it is to see how easily you were taken captive by a handful of men, and now you find yourself chained and sentenced to death. You have to know that my brother, Unay, is not isolated. The Cañaris, Chachapoyas, and Huaylas, are people who are numerous, well-armed, and have helped Unay. Now, unfortunately, they are paving the way for the foreigners.

- I have learned that not only from my men, but above all from the movement of the stars. A green and black comet, an omen of my death has been seen.

- Your mother is waiting for you in Quito. She believes she will see you alive because she remains uninformed of your true destiny.

- My body will be taken to Quito where I will rest among my people. I am not afraid of dying. I will be well cared for in the Hurin Pacha until I arrive at the Hanan Pacha, the realm of our god, Inti.

- You ordered the death of Unay, our brother, and you believed your generals when they told you it was accomplished. Well, it was not true. They deceived you into believing that they had tortured, harassed, and executed him, but they lied. Now the foreigners accuse you of having killed him, and it is one of the reasons they are using to justify the death penalty for you.

- How do you know all of this?

- Because my *chasquis* have kept me well-informed the entire time I was your mother's prisoner. Thank you for setting me free. Now I have to return to Cusco to see my family.

- Do you know where Unay is?

- I will never answer that question, no matter how you may torture or threaten to kill me.

- Were you tortured in Quito?

- Yes, on orders of your beloved mother, Tamaya.

- Unay is hidden, correct?

- Yes, happily he is in an undisclosed place. He is content, and has royal descendants, two children, to ensure his line of ancestry. The foreigners have no need to know this and I trust you, now that you are close to joining our father, you will keep your lips sealed about the news I have just given you.

- Who did Unay marry?

- I cannot answer that question, either.

- I think you just did. It has to be Kori. I knew they were friends from the time they were children, and it was always assumed that they would marry one day.

Killari remained quiet and looked at her brother with great sadness.

- You have the personality of a true leader Killari, and you would have been a good advisor alongside me. My men will not hurt you, and you are free to return to Cusco. I want you to know that our father kept me close to him from the time I was twelve years old. I would always accompany him on his journeys and war campaigns, and I learned everything I know from him. I was his favorite son and always felt the great love he had for me. He thought I was more capable of reigning because I understood the art of war.

- You are wrong, Tinkupuma. He wanted a shared government. From the time he was a child, Unay was prepared to govern Cusco, the capital of the Inca Empire and he understood that responsibility at a very early age. He preferred working and learning instead of playing because he took his responsibilities very seriously. I have personally witnessed all that I am telling you.

- I believe you, but the only certain thing is that I am sentenced to death and I am close to the end.

- Your generals are current on the events. That is why Rumiñahui has already taken it upon himself to divert the enormous treasure of gold toward Quito, and from there, to the mountains. He will hide it in secret caves, in order to save the Empire's riches.

- The foreigners are blinded by gold. They always deceived me, and never entertained setting me free. They are men without honor.

- I think they are coming for me. I'm sorry, I have to leave you in cruel hands.

- I hope you have a safe journey. Take care of yourself, sweet sister. My men will take you to Cusco and they will let you go from there to wherever you would like.

- Thank you. Have a good journey to the Hurin Pacha[21].

---

[21] Hurin Pacha - An afterlife place of the dead in Inca mythology.

Tinkupuma's sister had touched him deeply.

Legend says that his servants saw him crying golden tears, and when they dried, they turned into golden filigree. He was asked,

- Have you ever cried before?

- This is the first time, and it shall be the last.

The servants placed the golden filigree into a small vicuña fleece bag.

Chapter 32

Unay's warriors were in Sacsayhuaman. They were restless and nervous because of the long wait, contemplating that Anku's arrival should have been several hours earlier. Cusco had been plundered by the white men working day and night to dismantle the gold and silver in the precious Temples of the Sun and the Moon. The bodies of the past Emperors had already been moved to other places. There was no particular surveillance, with people coming and going in every direction. Unay's men guarded the deceased Emperor's body; it was not easy to discover it since the priests were on constant guard, day and night, at a distant site. The warriors had to convince the priests that Unay had ordered the removal of his father's embalmed body so that it might be transported from the Empire's capital. Anku was quite relieved when he realized that he could return immediately to Machu Picchu with the Emperor's body, and promptly begin searching for Killari.

Unay waited impatiently for the arrival of his father's body. He knew from the *chasquis* that Anku was on his way toward the hidden city of Machu Picchu. An elaborate ceremony to receive the body was planned and the High Priest was prepared. Rahua Ocllo, his widow, had cut her hair short as a sign of grief, and was preparing herself emotionally to receive her husband's remains. Kori readied her children and explained the meaning and importance of their grandfather's visitation, in a clear and simple manner.

The procession began immediately upon the early arrival of the late Emperor in Aguas Calientes. The body was placed on a royal palanquin and a hundred musicians played their percussion instruments, quenas, and zampoñas, harmoniously enhancing the great solemnity of the occasion. The melody was sad and and at the same time intense, creating a splendid musical balance. Just then two condors were observed flying across the heavens from Machu Picchu to Huayna Picchu causing Anku to reflect on Killari; he could not contain his tears. The Temple of the Sun was ready for the ceremony. Unay remained composed upon seeing his late father. Kori was beside him, holding the younger of their children in her arms. The couple's older child attentively observed the ceremony. The deceased was placed in the center of the Temple with his head facing toward Intihuatana. All in attendance prostrated themselves as a sign of respect for the sovereign Emperor, Unay's father, an unsurpassed man and warrior.

The High Priest eulogized the late Emperor, speaking of his government, conquests, great aqueduct, road, and bridge constructions, as well as his vast knowledge of the geography of the Empire and the art of war.

- We have seen two condors soaring across the sky of this city. It is a signal from the heavens informing us that our Emperor has been well-received by the Hanan Pacha, and now he is resting in peace here in Machu Picchu, the ancient mountain, a place in which he had always wanted to live. The spirits of the heavens are carrying him to his eternal life, to be with our God, the Sun.

The High Priest then signaled for everyone to bow down again as a sign of respect and spiritual farewell. After the ceremony ended, the musicians played uninterrupted, until nightfall.

Chapter 33

Unay summoned Anku to discuss the details of his journey.

- Have you any idea where Killari might be?

- Tamaya's soldiers kidnapped her. I suppose they are in Quito now.

- I think you should remain here. I will send my men to Quito to investigate the situation first. It is currently extremely unsafe to travel on the Empire's roads since too many hungry men are ready to attack anyone for a bit of food.

- It is impossible for me to just stand by idly. We are aware that Tinkupuma has been taken hostage in Cajamarca and has offered a large room filled with gold, and another with silver as his ransom. The white men do not respect our temples, our idols, or our gods. They are only hungry for gold and silver. They have convinced our peasants that their four-legged beasts, which they call horses, need to be fed gold and silver. The poor people accept this untruth because they have seen the horses bite a piece of metal, which the *viracochas* use to order the beasts in the direction they want them to go. I am fearful that Tamaya will release Killari to the foreigners and that they will also require a ransom for her.

- I have to recount something very serious to you. In the most recent skirmishes, our men were ambushed. Tinkupuma's generals observed a man they were certain was me, Unay. He was dressed in my clothes and looked very much like me. It was the strategy we had devised so that I would not be at risk in the event of an ambush. The worst part is, they imprisoned him and told my brother, Tinkupuma, of this capture. When they asked Tinkupuma about a strategy of treatment, my brother ordered them to kill the man, but torture and humiliate him first, in front of the soldiers. And so, they did. They forced him to drink urine and then quartered him and tossed him into the river. The man who impersonated me has a family and I have asked them to join us in Machu Picchu. They will live here with all the honors accorded the family of this martyr.

- I will depart for Quito without delay, but first I will visit Cajamarca to get fresh news about Tinkupuma.

- Be very careful. Go with the most trusted royal *chasquis;* they will keep me well-informed.

- Thank you, sir.

Chapter 34

Anku left quickly, anxious, thinking Killari could be dead at that very moment, or perhaps wounded from the torture she might have suffered forcing her to disclose Unay's location. Tamaya detested Killari and could inflict great pain on her, thought a worried Anku. He arrived at Cusco and considered resting there with his men. The city was unrecognizable after the desecration by the white men. He would have to wake up very early to continue the trek toward Cajamarca. The *chasquis* arrived, telling him that Tinkupuma would soon be executed, leaving the Empire without a ruler.

Anku awoke at dawn and set out accompanied by five of the foremost *chasquis*. At twilight, after a long hike, they noticed a group of armed men carrying a woman on a royal palanquin. Anku could not believe it was his beloved wife, Killari! He and his men concealed themselves in a bend of the road to protect themselves, because they had no idea of the intentions of the warriors. They knew they had to conceive of a way to talk to Killari, but remained hidden, allowing the other group to pass. Surely, they were en route to Cusco. Anku had no option but to follow at a distance, while remaining invisible to them until they observed Killari bidding farewell to these men and standing alone at the entrance to the city of Cusco. Anku was so nervous that he could barely speak. He told his premier *chasqui* to run to Killari and tell her that her husband was close by and that she should not leave. Killari saw the *chasqui* running toward her and waited, thinking he was bringing news of Tinkupuma's death. Anku saw Killari's enormous smile when the *chasqui* delivered the message from Anku. The two of them then ran to one another in the middle of the road and embraced. Anku held her in his arms, crying with joy. Suddenly Killari groaned due to the pain in her back.

- What's wrong, Killari? What hurts?

- My back. I still have some open wounds.

- Wounds? What happened?

- Tamaya ordered me to be tortured for several days, in an attempt to exact details about Unay's hiding place. I fabricated a story about the Sacred Valley, but they didn't believe me. Then I refused food and water because I feared they would poison me. After that, I don't remember anything, because they tell me that I fainted and was unconscious for some time.

- Why did Tamaya decide to let you go?

- It wasn't her. It was Tinkupuma. He was informed that I was a prisoner in Quito, and he ordered his mother to set me free and send me immediately to see him. I was very weak but Tamaya's healer attended to me and I was able to travel to Cajamarca. It was a difficult journey for me because of the pain of my wounds, but I was determined to speak with my brother.

- So, you saw him?

- Yes. It was a short meeting, but we told each other a lot of things in very little time. We recounted everything going on in the Empire and of his impending death.

- Is it true that they're going to execute him?

- I think they already have. We'll have to wait until the *chasquis* return with the news.

- We should take the route to Machu Picchu immediately. But we'll rest in the Sacred Valley. I know a place where we can be sheltered and fed. Then my *chasquis* will help carry you on the royal palanquin so that you can rest. From now on, I will watch over you as my little dove with broken wings.

- I will let myself be pampered. I miss my family and my people of Machu Picchu.

- We'll be there soon, love.

Chapter 35

Tinkupuma, who was sick with a fever, was given a tea made of *epazote* leaves to lower his temperature. He fell deeply asleep and dreamed that he was at the top of the volcano Cotopaxi with his mother. She said to him:

- You are safe with me, my son. No one will hurt you. The eternal fire will always protect us. We are close to Quito, your native land. This is your kingdom and you will rest here forever.

- No, mother. You are wrong. I have been made a prisoner of the foreigners who came from the sea. They have condemned me to death. I just want to ask you for one thing, that my soldiers take me to you, to Quito, and that my mummified body be placed looking eastward, where the sun rises.

- Be quiet. Do not speak of death. You are immortal. No one will hurt you while I am alive. You will be a father soon, and you will have descendants. I will always be beside you, taking care of you, so no one dare hurt you.

- Hold me, mother. Give me the strength to face an honorable death. I will teach these infidels, these dishonest and traitorous men a lesson.

- Stop talking nonsense. You are invincible, and nothing will happen to you. I assure you.

- I recall the story my beloved father told me. He was celebrating the Inti Raymi in Cusco when everyone saw a royal eagle being pursued by many hawks and falcons. It allowed itself to fall after it was attacked by the other birds. The High Priest said it was an ill-fated omen. It foretold the coming destruction of the Empire.

- My shaman tells me the opposite, that you will come to see me in Quito, and you will stay with me.

The figure of Tinkupuma's mother disappeared in a heavy mist. Then his brother Unay appeared to him, regally dressed and accompanied by Kori.

- What are you doing here in Cajamarca? You are already dead. My generals have assured me of it.

- Either they lied to you, or they believed that the man they killed was me. They were wrong. They killed a man who was impersonating me.

- What is my wife Kori doing here with you?

- Kori is my wife, and the mother of my children. She never belonged to you. Now we are safe in a beautiful place, close to the heavens, in an earthly paradise. There, we are untouchable. We will keep the heart of the Empire intact, and nobody will be able to find us. Tomorrow you will die, and they will bury you without having received our people's rites. That is your punishment for being so ambitious and refusing to accept our father's decision. You should have stayed in Quito with your mother.

- I have lost, and I accept my defeat and will not mourn the loss of my kingdom. Regardless, the Empire has suffered a lot and the foreigners are destroying our temples, our idols, and our religion. They are destroying our heritage, and nobody is stopping them.

- I will take care of preserving our culture and defending our people. My lineage will continue throughout time through my progeny.

As Unay and Kori disappeared from Tinkupuma's dream his father, the dead Inca, appeared. He was as he had been in his best years and he seemed worried.

- Father, have you come to be with me on the eve of my death?

- I have come to embrace you, because the love I have for you remains. You are still very young, and your inexperience overwhelmed you. You will always be my favorite child. You will not be able to confront the prophecy of the Viracocha. It will be fulfilled, and it will destroy our Empire, our culture, our people. I will be by your side at the moment of your death and will not abandon you. Tamaya, your mother, will receive your body and she will ensure that you are laid to rest as an Emperor in Quito.

- Now, I can die in peace father. Wait for me in the world of the dead. Stay with me until I walk the path leading me to the heavens, close to our God Inti.

Chapter 36

When Tinkupuma awakened, it was dawn. He heard shouting and arguing amongst the foreigners, and they told him that they could not agree on the manner of his death, or even whether it was necessary to kill him or leave him as a prisoner. Finally, they decided to kill him, and they told him so, for that night, he would die. Tinkupuma asked to see his women to give them instructions on preserving his body and sending it to Quito. His mother would make sure he was very well taken care of. It was essential that as soon as he was dead, they send a message to his mother telling her that she must wait for him, because he would soon arrive. However, his mother must not know about his death.

It was nighttime, the moment of execution had arrived, and he was moved to the central plaza. Tinkupuma argued with the bearded men because he did not want to die by fire, which would be counter to his ancient traditions. They decided to convert him to Christianity, their religion, and agreed that he would die by the garrotte, and not by fire. He accepted, and they baptized him with the name Juan Francisco. Then they killed him immediately. It was practically an assassination, because all the charges against him had been completely fabricated, or at least they had no proof of them. They included idolatry, incest, murder of his brother Unay, the true Ruler of the Empire, as well as usurping the job of the Emperor. The list was very long. Worst of all, the person who was translating between Quechua and Spanish was a native of the north who hated Tinkupuma. In addition, the translator had already set his sights on one of the prisoner's wives and he would not consider allowing Tinkupuma to live and stay with her.

Tinkupuma died by the garrotte, strangled. They burned his hair and brought him to a building that was used as a church by the Conquistadors. They buried him in secret, but within a few days his body disappeared. It is said that the leader of the bearded men cried bitterly when Tinkupuma was executed. He had taken a liking this ruler, and the guilt he felt remained with him until the end of his days. Tinkupuma was quite smart. He had not only learned many of their games, such as chess, but he always managed to win. He had also learned some of the language of the invaders. The foreigners allowed his wives to visit and take care of him. When they learned of the death of Tinkupuma, his wives asked to be executed and buried beside him. The foreigners tried to prevent suicides, but they could not prevent all of them, since some of his wives strangled themselves with their braids.

Chapter 37

Tinkupuma's warriors kidnapped his body. Since they knew the geography of the area better than anyone, they could transport it easily. They arrived in Quito and announced to Tamaya that her son was coming to see her. Tamaya dressed in her nicest garments and adorned herself with her most precious jewels to receive him. The generals presented themselves.

- Where is my son, the Emperor?

- He is on his way, but you must prepare yourself to see him with different eyes.

- I do not understand you. Has he arrived in Quito? Is he sick? Hurt?

- Let the Emperor Tinkupuma pass through, announced one of the generals in a raised voice.

The servants cleared the path where the Emperor would pass. The royal golden palanquin bore Tinkupuma seated in a large chair, dressed in his finest regalia. Tamaya could not believe what she was seeing. Her son's eyes were closed, and he neither moved nor spoke. It was as if he were dead.

- What has happened to our Emperor? Answer me, fools! screamed Tamaya, beside herself.

- The foreigners we call *viracochas* have killed him, breaking their promise to set him free as soon as they received the treasure for his ransom.

- And you, what have you done? Why did you not defend him? The army of the Emperor has thousands of warriors and, according to what I have been told, the foreigners are only a few men, Tamaya demanded, furiously.

- It was his destiny, my lady, *Coya*. You must accept the prophecy of the *Viracocha,* as the priests explained when the spirits of the Temple were questioned. They have seen it clearly in the entrails of the sacrificed llamas. They have seen the same green comet that Tinkupuma's father saw, which announced the destruction and the death of our civilization.

- We have followed the orders of our lord Tinkupuma at every moment. At the beginning, he thought that he would be set free.

- Get out, everyone! Leave me alone with my son! yelled Tamaya, beyond upset.

Everyone left, and Tamaya approached her son. She noticed that his hair had been burned. He had already been embalmed. She began to talk to him as if he were still alive.

- Nobody will hurt you. You will stay with me forever. We will travel throughout the Empire of the four *suyos*. We will bathe in the waterfalls of Baños. We will journey to the coast to watch the immensity of the sea. We will listen to the sound of the conch-shell trumpets announcing our royal arrival in each town. We will climb the highest mountains close to our great Lord Inti. We will see the great rivers carve the earth of the Andes with their fierce currents. Our animals will accompany us, and nobody will trouble us. The gods will be by our side with their great power and nobody will harm us. Look, my son, upon my great beauty, which you have inherited. We are immortal. We are the divine, eternal race.

Upon announcing these words, Tamaya fainted.

The servants found Tamaya unconscious and with a high fever. She was delirious. The healer told all the ladies-in-waiting that she should drink herbal tea to lower her fever. These servants continuously attended to her all night long, trying to revive the *Coya*. In a few days' pustules began to appear on her body. Tamaya remained delirious; she shouted out and scratched herself ripping her skin. Her attendants tied her hands so that she would not destroy her flesh with her fingernails. Tamaya called for her son to come and take her with him to the volcano Cotopaxi, and further told him that all the pumas would accompany them, and no one would dare to harm them as the spirits of the netherworld were with them. The sickness lasted for one month. With the fine care of her servants, Tamaya survived. The day she recovered consciousness and was able to eat solid food, she asked to be stripped naked and bathed. The women who accompanied her refused, saying that her skin was still very damaged and that she must wait. Just then, Tamaya touched her face and noticed something strange. She asked for her silver mirror to see herself. The servants demurred, indicating that the mirror had been lost. Tamaya became very angry and demanded that they give her the mirror. They obeyed fearfully. Upon seeing herself in the mirror, Tamaya saw that the disease, the same illness that had killed her late husband, had disfigured her face. The pustules had left pockmarks on her face, and her beauty had disappeared. Now she was a *Coya* forever bearing the stamp of an unknown disease. She called for herbs to help her sleep. The year of mourning for Tamaya's son was passed thusly in Quito.

Chapter 38

Killari and Anku arrived in Machu Picchu. Unay had been expecting their arrival for a few days based on reports from the chaquis and waited for them excitedly with Kori and his mother, Rahua Ocllo, the *Coya* of the Empire. He was dressed in a white tunic, *uncu*[22] that reached his knees, and was made of the best cotton. Across his shoulders there was a draped cape called *yacolla*. His coca leaves were carried in sacks, *chulpas*. When Killari and Anku arrived, the sister and brother embraced.

- Finally, you're here. We went through great anguish when we heard that you had been arrested by Tamaya's men and taken to Quito.

- Yes, brother. At that time, I thought I might die without seeing you or my beloved husband Anku again.

- I was told that you were tortured for many days.

- It's true, but I have been protected by my Goddess the Moon.

- I have seen the wounds, and they are serious. We must continue treating them, said Anku.

- I will do it myself, said Killari's mother.

- I see you are pregnant again, said Killari, smiling.

---

[22] Uncu - Inca men's tunic, in standardized format, dimensions, and construction.

- That's right. I'm the happiest woman every time I learn I am with child. We have to ensure a line of succession for our Empire, said Kori.

- Come in and rest. We will talk later about the most recent events, said Unay.

Killari left with her mother to treat the wounds, and to bring her current on all that had transpired since her departure.

After a few hours the family came together again to eat. Each one had a plate of soft corn called *capia*. The bread, *tanta,* was also made of corn. There were potatoes, *chuño* (a special preparation of potato), *apichu* or sweet potato, gourds, avocados, and the meat of *cuy*, or guinea pig, as well as *taruka*, an Andean deer. For dessert they had several kinds of fruit, including a flavorful sweet fruit called *cuchuchu*, eggfruit, pepino melon, guava or *pacay,* bananas, and pineapples.

Then they retired to their private quarters. The only people present were the family, Unay, Kori, Killari, Anku, and the *Coya* Rahua Ocllo.

- We have news from Cajamarca. TInkupuma has been executed by what the foreigners call a garrotte, which is a strangling apparatus. His body has been taken to Quito where Tamaya resides. She became ill with the same disease that killed my father. Nevertheless, she survived, but it left her terribly pockmarked, and her legendary beauty has vanished. Now we must deal with a bigger issue. The foreigners believe they have eliminated both Tinkupuma, the usurping Emperor, and Unay, the legitimate heir. The truth is that I am alive, and I have children to perpetuate our Empire, thanks to our God Viracocha, affirmed Unay.

- The priority is rebuilding our army, but we must stay here in the Hidden City, responded Anku.

- I agree with my husband. Tinkupuma gave the order to avoid confrontation with the foreigners, and so, many tribes envision recapturing the independence they once enjoyed. They are helping the white men, and I have personally observed it. The *Llayca*[23] of the Empire has reminded us of the vision our father experienced when he returned from one of the Empire's northern conquests. A moon was seen, surrounded by three circles; the first was red representing the blood spilled in the war between brothers; the second was black, representing the destruction of our religion and the plagues that would kill so many, and finally the circle made of smoke, symbolizing the destruction of the Empire. The events of the red circle have already occurred, and now we see the consequences. The black circle omen is occurring as we speak. We must avoid the prediction of the circle of smoke from happening. We cannot let our Inca Empire disappear, said Killari, passionately.

- The Empire has received a direct assault and it is gravely injured. The effect of these white foreigners will be seen very soon. They are coming from another very distant place, with another king, and from what I have heard, they are exceedingly greedy for gold and silver. They have dismantled our temples and profaned our mummies and sacred *huacas*. That destruction is complete, and there is no going back. Now we must retreat to gain strength and determine how to better defend ourselves, concluded Rahua Ocllo.

- You're very right, mother. You have always given good advice. This is the right time for our retreat, so that we may better take up the reins of our Empire again. Our people need to know we exist, but for the time being we cannot disclose our whereabouts. In this hidden city we will continue our traditions, adore our gods, and educate our children so that they will also love our people and protect them, said Unay.

---

[23] Llayca - Medicine man or shaman.

- I have seen Killari's wounds and many of them have already scarred over, but there will always be marks on her back. They form an almost perfect picture of a condor with open wings. It is a good sign for us. The condor is an intelligent bird and it belongs to the heavenly world of the gods. Thus, we will be protected as governors and as a family, said Killari's mother.

- You must have suffered greatly when they whipped you with those ropes that had points covered with gold, said an emotional Anku.

- It's true, but I never disclosed the location of Machu Picchu, so now we can enjoy our refuge for many years.

- Now it's our turn to have a family, said Anku tenderly.

- Let's hope that the family grows to strengthen the Empire and increases our happiness, said Unay.

Killari and Anku had five children, three boys and two girls. They educated them according to the Inca culture, filling them with the fundamental qualities of justice and tolerance. They lived in absolute peace and seclusion in Machu Picchu for the rest of their days, preparing themselves for the return of the glorious Inca Empire. One of them was the great-grandfather of Tupac Amaru, the successor of the Inca dynasty. But that is another story.

Printed by Amazon Italia Logistica S.r.l.
Torrazza Piemonte (TO), Italy